AKHAND HIND FAUJ

PRASAD DESHPANDE

Made with ♥ on the Notion Press Platform
www.notionpress.com

Contents

Contents

Foreword

Author's Fore-Word:

As usual, the statutory warning...

This work is entirely fiction and any resemblance to anyone, any place or any incidence is purely a coincidence – or – maybe, your wild imagination... J

Reader Warning: This story contains extreme violence and murders. People with weak hearts/mind & children are advised to keep away from it.

I started writing this story and the story of **Disposables** somewhere in Feb 2022 – unfortunately, I had a health problem and had to take complete rest toward the end of 2022. Else, this story along with *Disposables* would have been published at the end of last year...

'Disposables' was published April 2023 and this will get probably in June / July of 2023.

India gained its Freedom with lots and lots of sacrifices by its Freedom fighters. Many gave up their families and lavish lives to realise this dream. Many gave up their lives – e.g. Lala Lajpatrai, Bhagat Singh, Chandrashekhar Azad, Ashfaqullah, Ramprasad Bismil and millions of unidentified, unrecognized Indians.

Netaji Subhashchandra Bose led an army of patriots known as **Azad Hind Fauj**...

They all had one dream – Free and Independent India.

Nobody of them dreamed of a partition. Nobody dreamed about strife. They all wanted entire India to be together – **Akhand Bharat**... and they wanted it to flourish...

Switch to post Y2K and Covid – The state of politics has gone down to its lowest level. People are wondering and wanting to know the real truth. There are traitors who want to further disintegrate this wonderful nation into pieces. The media cannot be trusted. The leaders cannot be trusted. The legal proceedings are under doubt of favouritism. People are divided in groups and against each other. Someone has to do something about it...

"**AKHAND HIND FAUJ**" may soon be a reality considering the state of affairs in the nation ... Indian people and politicians have to realise this, sooner, the better ...

CHAPTER ONE

One

It was hot and dry in the desert of Rajasthan. The police were taking a traitor and a mafia don who was a political leader from a jail in Rajasthan to a court in Delhi. The people in favour of that traitor feared that he would be killed by police in the transit or an accident would be made to happen killing him instantly. So was the media who wanted to capture such an occurrence...

The crazy media in quest of TRP was following the caravan of the police in bid to see if that would happen and claim that they were the first to report it on the TV. Most of them were covering it LIVE...

Priya Singhal was a glamorous and a pretty TV Journalist. She was one of the reporters covering this event with her newly joined cameraman 'Chaitanya'. He was bored by all this nonsense reporting but it was his job to do so – he was tagging along. He wanted to be a daring cameraman who would shoot some perilous scenes and earn his name and fame.

The caravan stopped at a dhaba by the highway for food and rest. So did the crazy journalists and reporters. They were not allowed to interact or interview the traitor. They had their food and rested and whiled away their time. It was boring...

Suddenly some masked people stopped by in two cars and opened up fire on the resting police. There was a scramble of these journalist and reporters to get to a safe place and then report the happenings. Priya started to run towards safety but found Chaitanya missing. She saw him in thick of firing, his camera turned ON and shooting the proceeding.

"Come to safety and shoot the happening..." she shouted out to Chaitanya but he was beyond the reach of her voice and kept on shooting the scene with his camera. The police hadn't had a chance as the attack was sudden, quick and in an organized manner. They approached the traitor and shot at him spraying hell lot of bullets – killing him instantly ... none of the policemen were killed or hurt...

One of their bullets shattered his camera. While the tyres of police cars and the press vans were flattened by them shooting the bullets at them...

"You are crazy." she said looking aghast at Chaitanya – "you could've got killed in all that firing. Safety comes first then the reporting. Along with you, I will get killed one day."

Chaitanya laughed, "Don't you worry – in such a circumstance; I will ensure that your safety is taken care of first. See – nothing has happened to you or me... I took a calculated risk... and we are the only ones who have the close footage of this attack."

"Your camera is shattered." she pointed out.

"But, the recording disk isn't. I still have the recording on the DVD." he smiled.

She gave a huge sigh of relief and said "Now the media has weeks of discussions as to how this attack was put into action and who could have behind it. I think – I will have to be in studio conducting those boring debates where people with no knowledge keep yapping."

"Suits you... You are not made for this tough action."

She put out a tongue to tease him and laughed, "Let's be on our way to Delhi and our studio..."

CHAPTER TWO

Two

It was a typical sweaty evening of Mumbai. He strolled out of the theatre satisfied that he had tried his best. He smiled at the mixed reaction of the audience from the general public.

He smiled at the fact that he was branded as an Urban Naxal. He always had projected himself as a Stand-up Comedian (he was not – he knew his jokes were sick and aimed at a particular leader).Through his so called comedy, all he did was to make fun of ruling parliamentary party not realising that he was targeting a popular Prime Minister of India and the leaders who were with him. Along with killing the image of the Prime Minister, he also was trying to create a rift among masses and turning them against each other...

He never was concerned about his earnings from his shows and acts – his main income was undisclosed amount of favours from the opposition party members. They paid him these huge amounts, so that he can dirty the popular image of the Prime Minister and let the people remember him as a joke instead...

It was supposed to be a slow poison injected in the populace and the society – all this only to be able to rule the Golden Nation called – **Hindustan**.

He lit up an expensive cigar and casually walked toward the car – a service offered by a member of an opposition party.

"Good evening Sir..." the driver greeted him.

"Where's Raju – he was the driver who brought me here." he said looking at a different person greeting him near the car.

"He's left for the day. We work in shifts. His shift is done with ... I'm here at your service."

"Oh! What's your name?"

"I'm Anil. Would you like to go straight to the guest house or enjoy some night life in Mumbai?"

"I want some fresh breeze and sip on a chilled beer."

"I understand – let me drive you to such a place."

"Mind you – it shouldn't be crowded."

"Right Sir..." and they started to cruise the roads of Mumbai – fabulously lit up with various hoardings adding to the glamour of the city. The car stopped in front of a wine shop and required bottles were bought – in the meantime Anil got a parcel of chicken nuggets fabulously spiced up and its aroma spread around in the car – it was from a nearby roadside stall, but deliciously cooked.

"Hmm – the smell is nice. I now understand why they have you at the night shift – Anil, I hope you are much more efficient than you look..."

Anil picked up the cue..."If you want to pick up a chick enroute to the guest house – I know few fabulous girls – let me know when we head back to the guest hose..." and they drove on. They stopped on a beach that was almost desolate at the odd hours. They drove into the sand of the beach and stopped. It was ebb time.

He got out of the car and filled in his lungs with whiff of fresh sea breeze that rejuvenated him. He pulled out a bottle from the car and started to sip at it and looked at Anil...

"You seem to be efficient enough – let me see which girls are on your list..."

"You want a glamorous doll or someone who is simple but sexy?"

"You got it – I heard you have many girls who are lookalike of famous female stars and personalities..."

As an answer Anil pulled out his phone and showed him a picture – a girl – almost similar to a hot actress – then started to scroll on for more such girls – he stopped at a wave of hand...

"Could you fix her for me?"

"Hey – I got you a customer – you ready for the jazz?" Anil called someone up from his phone and started to deal, "Don't worry about anything – I got the deal fixed – he is a famous personality. Don't worry about the payment – it will be taken care of as usual. I'll send you the location on your phone..." he looked at the so called comedian who now was sitting sideways, his feet dangling outside, on the back seat with door open, sipping at another bottle of beer, "The deal is ON – she is yours for the night..." he smiled wide at the comedian, "I now want you to close your eyes for a moment and imagine how fabulous is going to be this night..."

The so called comedian somehow liked this idea and closed his eyes and started to imagine ... after a moment he opened his eyes which were full of lust. This was momentary, the lust vanished and expression of horror took over. He was looking at a nozzle of a gun fitted with silencer – Anil held that gun...

"Wha..." he started even as Anil shot him between his eyes – point blank...

Next morning, police found the car almost a feet deep in the tide. Driver Raju was found alive drugged and sedated in the boot of the car. There were no clues leading to this mysterious murder...

CHAPTER THREE

THREE

It was a hot afternoon in Kerala. Members of a belligerent group MFI had gathered for planning further action toward their group ideology. They were closely linked with ISIS. One of their top leaders was addressing them. The group was of about 15 persons. They took a break from their meeting – "See why the lunch is being served so late – we have to carry on with this meeting till all points are discussed..."

It was a farm house and was secluded. It had a tight security by MFI's own armed members. It was secluded in green thickness of Kerala. It was normally used to plan some decisive action that they were about to take – especially the belligerent faction of the group.

They were planning to use the Bangladeshi and the Rohingya fugitives living in various parts of India to create arson and disrupt the peace in the nation. They wanted to destroy the very fabric of social acceptance in India.

They wanted to use them and impress upon the muslims living in India that the current government is against them and they need to reciprocate the hate spread by the government – it was not true, but, it was a perception they wanted to create. They knew if they could use these fugitives, the public anger will automatically be on the muslims who lived in peace and brotherhood and sometime will reach a point where they will be forced to take up local arms in resistance to this movement by the fugitives. This would be responded by muslims in self-defence...

A group paramilitary force commandos – that's what it looked like, was approaching stealthily towards that location. They were careful enough not to be seen or noticed by anyone from the security force of MFI. They moved in with a plan and in a planned manner.

At a precise time – they attacked the place silencing the guard by the MFI's security using their knives. In few minutes, the entire guard was eliminated. Few of them stealthily moved toward the place where documents were kept – it seemed they knew the place very well.

While others encircled the hall where this meeting was on and waited for the move. Few kept vigil for anyone approaching the premise and few went around the premise killing the staff and others who could raise an alarm.

The leader of that mission showed a sign that in 1 minute they would force into the meeting hall and everyone braced for the action. They knew that this group could possess arms and were cautious. The attack had to be sudden and precise.

It was a sudden attack – the force invaded from the windows and the main door. They killed everyone except 3 people who were the top planners of the group. Before they could realise what had happened – they were surrounded and abducted.

The force left with those 3 people and the documents they were looking for as quietly as they had appeared at the premise. Nobody around a mile knew that such an operation had been a success. Around evening, when one of its members visited, the action on the scene was discovered...

The local police were baffled as to who could have done this act of crime and started to investigate the matter. There were at least 50 people killed and they didn't know how many more were going to be killed. During investigation one of the locals told them that he had seen a vehicle with cadres who looked like they were from CRPF or military around the vicinity at the time.

The army denied any such action and the government knew that CRPF or the military was not activated by them for this reason. Then who could have carried out this massacre??

CHAPTER FOUR

FOUR

Normal day in Chennai and everything was normal. About 185 kms off Chennai at a beach fishermen were busy they had had a good catch of fish and were happy that after a lot many days they had such a good catch.

Recently their catch had gone down because some fishing trawlers had been visiting the sea and gobbling up their catch of fish. They had tried to raise their voice to authorities to cancel the permits of the trawlers in their area and ask them to fish in deep sea – all on deaf ears.

They were planning a protest march to the local Fisheries department to put out their demands and get rid of the trawlers. They made banners and leaflets which they could distribute to local people for gathering help.

They saw the trawlers returning from deep sea. These trawlers were not seen during the day while they collected a huge catch. The trawlers belonged to strong armed musclemen and they were afraid to confront them directly. The trawlers were hardly about half a nautical mile away when huge blasts were seen on those trawlers.

They couldn't believe their eyes and the blasts were really huge. The blasts started to sink the trawlers and they rushed in with their small boats to rescue the people on board of the trawlers. They were able to save almost everyone – a few who were injured in the blasts couldn't make it.

Nobody was sure how these blasts had occurred. The local authorities were informed who started an investigation in the matter. They were supposed to be fishing trawlers and nobody bothered to check for any material loss. In about 2 days the debris started to gather on the shore and a box was found. It contained banned drugs.

This became a knowledge as one of the reporters happened to notice it and spread the word around through his media channel. Now everyone was asking questions and the owner of the trawlers was absconding. There was a drug business involved and the narcotics department got involved.

They called in professional divers to explore and retrieve whatever they could salvage from the wrecks below the sea. What they found alerted the entire system. There were boxes containing arms and ammunition and loads of fake currency which could destabilize the nation... similar blast incidences happened on the coasts of Andhra Pradesh and Orissa – and they too were being probed – they also were sunk and were carrying similar shipments.

A manhunt was lodged to arrest the owners of these trawlers. But, they kept evading. Some were believed to have travelled to other nations who did not have extradition treaty with India and were safe. While those who couldn't were being hunted for and were running around to escape the hand of the law.

Few were arrested but nobody knew what happened after that – the cases remained untold stories... from the so called happenings media also moved on to other stories which yielded them TRP...

CHAPTER FIVE

The protestors had gathered at Shivamogga in Karnatak. They were shouting slogans against the government's lack of response towards the issues of the common man. The state government belonged to the ruling party –the party who ruled the Central government but was involved in their petty politics.

The youth leader who led the protests was from the party that ruled the central government – against his own party and was facing lots of snags because of the opposition party tantrums which were baseless. The opposition party only wanted the government to fall so that they can bid to form an alternate government.

There were elements in the opposition party who were downright crafty and used common people to create trouble. They also had links with goons and underworld to carry out their nefarious activities. One such party worker from one of the opposition party was watching these protests with keen interest... He was not from the main opposition party in the state – this was a third opposition party.

This was the third day of the protest and things were getting ugly. The protestors had damaged the cars of the ruling state government officials and the protest seemed to get more and more response from the general public who had started to join it en masse.

The evening saw tremendous crowd join the protest and the procession carrying banners of “Down with the government”. The state government was at a loss to curb this protest – obviously, it had done something wrong and for benefit of its own leaders.

The opposition party worker from the third opposition party who was watching this made a call and a band of hooligans arrived on the site and started to vandalize around. Nobody could make out the hooligans from the crowd and all started to get involved in arson as the rage in the crowd was raised and the effect of hooliganism had its effect on the crowd.

The state police had to call in more cops in emergency – they first started to use tear gas shells and water cannons to disperse the crowd. The person watching the on-going clash between the police and the crowd signalled to a group in police as well as few hooligans – and they opened up fire on the crowd. The order for fire was not given by the state – this was being done on his signal. He was from one of those parties who wanted to have a stronghold in the region and these policemen and hooligans were hired by that party...

Everything went haywire. He wanted to create rift in the crowd that was united. In the melee that ensued, he signalled to one of his hooligan and they formed a group and approached the youth leader leading the protest. He was trying to calm down the crowd. The hooligans encircled the youth leader and stabbed him many times to his death on the spot. This created a further uproar in the crowd.

The leader and the party member from the third opposition party had achieved what they wanted. Now the crowd was split and started to blame one sect of society and started to wage violence against them. The media reporters were in glee at the turn of events and were busy in interviewing people from different sects about the murder of the leader – thus furthering the cause of the third opposition party – creating the rift in united crowd... They were getting their TRP.

The third opposition party had now started to gather the respect and the mandate of the crowd and were becoming belligerent to get more seats in the ministry – this would not only strengthen the party's stand but also allow them to be corrupt at high level and gather party funds.

The person who had engineered the rift in crowd by killing the youth leader was crossing a busy road in Bangalore. He saw the traffic was fast but thick – he was jaywalking to cross the road and somehow reached the centre divider of the road.

He looked at the other side of thick and fast traffic when his eyes showed horror. Two people on a motorcycle were almost close to him at a high speed – and suddenly, a sword flashed from the man behind. The motorcycle passed close to him and in one sweep of the sword – he lay beheaded on the divider. The traffic was thick and fast – nobody noticed at first what had happened and by the time they realised – the motorcycle had vanished...

The small leader of that third opposition party who had been this person's guide resided at Bellary and was at peace awaiting the next instruction from the central leadership located at Delhi. He was addressing a small meeting of his party workers and in a daring attack was shot dead while others from his party were left injured.

This was portrayed by media as a rivalry of competition of various opposition parties at the local level leading the investigation in a wrong direction. The media and the people forgot these incidences as other **Breaking News** gripped the nation...

CHAPTER SIX

SIX

Switching back to Rajasthan ...

In Delhi - The NSA called Mr Mahal who was the chief of Special Security Force of IB. They discussed the various incidences in detail and were half convinced that these were connected. They were yet unsure that there was a connection between these – they were spread all across India and it had to be a huge and organised effort to carry them out.

Who could run such an organized killing all over India? Who could be behind such an organized operation pan India? The thought was insane at the same time it was alarming. If somebody had managed to form a group that could operate all over the nation and yet remain unknown was a danger signal. They could do anything, create any sort of trouble and take control of the nation.

This couldn't be done without collecting internal individuals with vested interests like money and power. Further, most of the people who were killed were against the central ruling party. Can central ruling party have a hand in these of crimes? Obviously, it suited them as their adversaries were being eliminated one by one...

The other problem was this group of people had killed members who were lesser known politicians, influencers and hooligans who belonged to various opposition parties.

Were these separate incidences or was someone pulling the strings to make these happen??

Or could this be an act of an opposition political party who wanted to destabilize the current government to grab power at the centre... Or could it be that some external power like Pakistan be involved in destabilizing the country... The incidences were happening in India and so the concern...

Mr Mahal already had anticipated this investigation and had started placing his agents belonging to IS and IB in various parties and other social platforms. He made sure that they were well covered up. He also had some of his commandos in IB posted in various fields he thought were sensitive and could be dangerous in this mission – after all – people were being killed and in a professional manner – no clues left behind...

He knew of few reporters who were highly patriotic and will be difficult to sell out and asked them to keep a watch on anything that may be suspicious or outright treachery. Priya Singhal was one of those journalists who he could trust. She also had a wide network of informers at her disposal and had been of help when needed. She had worked for IB in such cases where sensitivity was a prime concern. Even she didn't have any idea that this was the case IB was thinking to be a nationwide threat... He was yet to speak to her.

Then this happened – the traitor of a leader and a mafia don was murdered by unknown masked group who attacked and killed when he was being brought to Delhi for trial. The attack seemed extremely army professional and that had raised further alarm bells in the IB and NSA... He was a leader in one of the opposition parties.

Priya and Chaitanya started to move back to Delhi and their studio. It was a long journey and it was almost evening. They had a choice of stopping at a hotel in Jaipur and proceeding to Delhi next day. They took the option to stop over and rest before a hard day at the studio. They booked into a hotel and had their dinner. They said bye for the night and disappeared into their respective rooms. Next day, they proceeded to Delhi. They were travelling back extremely bored because that mafia don was dead and there was no other news than speculation...

"Hey stop the car." she called out to the driver.

"Now – what's the matter?" Chaitanya asked her stifling a yawn.

"Nothing I want to stretch my legs – they are cramped."

"Okay – let's get out of the car."

They got out of the car and looked at the stretch of desert. Nothing except sand and few scattered bushes could be seen...

"Let's explore this part of desert a bit..." she said taking a water bottle from the car, "that'll enable some walk and stretch the legs further."

"In this heat?"

"Ya – why not – let's go..."

He shrugged and followed her keeping his damaged camera in the car. They walked straight into the desert about a mile when she gave a mischievous smile. He didn't see that smile and kept walking beside her – deep in thought as to who could have carried out such a daring assassination of the leader cum mafia don. Could it be some rival group?

"Let me do some modelling." she said suddenly, "click some great pictures of me – I want to upload them on Instagram..."

"Are you crazy? In this heat you want to do some modelling? Can't you find some beautiful spot and get your modelling done there?" the chain of his thoughts was broken.

"Come on – you are a photographer and look at me – am I not pretty and hot?"

"I don't know about you but the Sun is pretty hot."

"Don't be a spoil sport – click some pictures of me as if I am reporting from this desert. They would make great posts on Instagram..."

"Why are you girls so obsessed with Instagram?" he mused.

"Click some pictures – I will also mention that you as a cameraman clicked these pictures and give you the credit and followers..."

"I'm not on any of social media platforms. I hate them. All false friends – nobody true you can rely on..."

"But I love to be socially active – just don't think – click them."

He shrugged again and started to click her photos on his mobile. He was irritated as she wanted to look at every picture he clicked and decide whether to keep it or delete it.

"From a cameraman's perspective – we will have to go in a bit further into the desert and the background of that mound there will give you the perfect clicks you want and would like to be framed in..."

"Okay let's go in a bit further as you suggest." and they walked in still deeper till they were about half a furlong from the mound he had pointed. He asked her to stand in front of the mound and clicked some pictures which she approved. He was about to the click next one when he could see a faint smouldering smoke behind her.

"Hey what's that smoke? It seems to be coming from behind you. Who could be burning something in this burning heat of the desert?"

"Come on – let's find out..." she said, the investigative journalist in her coming to the fore.

They quickly covered the ground till the mound and started to climb it even as the smoke started to increase in its density as if something was set on fire. They climbed on the mound and to their horror saw 2 vans on fire. The third van started to drive away with brooms attached near its tyres so as to wipe out any tyre marks. The brooms were tied with a cloth which not only held the brooms but also covered the number plate of the van.

They quickly moved towards them to see if anyone was in those vans to be saved. There was nobody in the vans on fire...

"Priya! These are those vans which were used by the attackers yesterday. They are trying to erase their identity by putting these vans on fire." and he started to click the pictures of the burning vans.

"Why are you clicking the so many pictures of these vans – one is enough for us to report it on TV..."

"You want to be an investigative journalist – right? This is your chance. We have to get clues to this event and push the investigation harder to know who was behind the killing – will be a great name for you – Priya Singhal the best investigative journalist ... what say ..."

She dreamed of the accolades for a moment, "You are right ... let's begin the investigation on this matter – on our own. I am with you."

"Good girl. Now take that branch and break the window glass open – let's see if we can manage to get the view inside the burning van."

They tried in vain to take some pictures of the interiors but were unable as the fire raged still further. He realised that the van's fuel tanks were close to the fire – he grabbed her hand and started to run. They had run far enough when the vans blasted throwing them off balance and they hit the sandy ground hard. They got up and brushed themselves off and watched the remnants of those vans burn and char.

They walked back to their car and called the police as good citizens that they had heard a blast in the desert. Then the car cruised on toward Delhi without any further incident.

CHAPTER SEVEN

SEVEN

Once in Delhi, they looked at the photographs and decided to investigate. She came over to his simple flat that he had rented. She realized that she knew nothing about Chaitanya. He was staying in a rented flat and his family seemed somewhere in Maharashtra. He was there for a journalistic career.

She came from a decent family background located in Bihar. Her father was a principal in a college and had supported her journey to journalism. She had no siblings and many cousins. They were all proud to watch her on the TV.

She sported bouncy hair long enough to touch her lower back – mostly wavy and used to treat it to form curls toward the end. She used to sport tight blouse and a skirt or trousers normally divided by a designer belt. This portrayed her to be a glamorous doll of a news presenter but she had an intelligent brain to match her looks. She dreamed of being an investigative journalist. She had a good network of informers to support her journalistic endeavour and aspirations.

She wanted to know more about him but he was completely devoted to work and did not talk about himself. He was fun but his fun was limited to his work. He was caring and compassionate – she remembered that he had helped a poor ragged man from an accident – not just looked at him and clicked pictures for his reporting. He was strong and had a muscular build as if he overworked his muscles everyday but was kind and spent lot of his earnings to buy food for poor people who couldn't afford to buy their meals.

He was a kind of mysterious – never showed any of his emotions. She was in his flat which was simple, No photos of family – in fact no photos hanging on the wall. There was one big quartz clock hanging on the wall. A simple kitchen with nominal utensils to prepare tea / coffee and to hold milk, He had subscribed to tiffin that was delivered daily.

"What do you think? Where should we start this investigation? Any leads or ideas?" she said settling down on the sofa.

"No leads – but I have been able to capture the number plates of those vans before they were charred. Let's begin there – at least we will know who the owner is of those vans... They look like Bihar number plates."

"Oh! Bihar – I have a friend in RTO over there – I can ask him without telling why I want the details of those number plates." she dialled a number, "show me photos of those number plates..." and he clicked on them showing her the number plates, "Hey Rakesh – long time that we have met. No – no – I am still in Delhi. How are you and how is your family?"

She listened to what so called Rakesh was saying. Then she bit her lip and asked him about the vehicle registered in Bihar with number plates that Chaitanya showed her..."okay then, let me know when you find out. No – no – This is routine reporting work..."

"He will let us know in about few minutes. I wonder who in Bihar would be interested in killing this gangster of a leader." she said and started waiting for Rakesh's call. He got up and went into the kitchen to prepare a coffee for both of them.

They were sipping on the coffee when her phone buzzed.

"Hey – Rakesh – what's the news? – sure? – Just hold on for a moment..." she turned toward Chaitanya, "Those vans seem to be owned by the Additional Superintendent of Police, Bihar..."

"Ask him if they are missing?"

"Are they missing by any chance? – you sure – ok, thanks for that information – see you when I visit Bihar..."

Looking at Chaitanya's expression of what now – she broke the news to him, "The vans are very much in Bihar. He travelled in one of those and is attending his office. The other van is still parked in his office premise – makes no sense."

"They must have used his van's number plates. They were phoney. They must have done this deliberately to lead the investigation to Bihar – but it beats me why his vans?"

"Obviously – they wanted to play safe- no clues left – right? Come on let's go to our office – work to do as well we will come to know if anyone else or some other channel has a breakthrough in this matter..."

They reached their office. She had no assignment and the news presentation was already decided for other presenters. While one cameraman was absent due to some medical emergency at his home, Chaitanya was asked to be a shift-in cameraman. It was a boring assignment where they had to cover a press conference of a local leader who was against the central government. It was known what matters he would be speaking on and what questions he would raise.

She sat in the office preparing a report on what happened in Rajasthan when her phone buzzed – it was Mr Mahal. She left the office to meet him on his request. If Mr Mahal had called her, it must be something important... She reached his office and was made to sit at the reception. The guy at the reception looked at her and was trying to impress her while she gazed through some newspapers.

She was called in to his cabin. There was nobody except Mr Mahal in the cabin, "Sit – I have something important to discuss" he said lighting up his pipe. He put a file in front of her and asked her to look it up. It contained all the killings that had recently happened in India, right from the comedian in Mumbai, to massacre in Kerala to blasts in Tamilnadu, Orissa and Andhra Pradesh. The file also had other killings in Assam, Bihar, Punjab, Kashmir and Madhya Pradesh. She read the file and looked at him in wonder as to what he was trying to imply...

"What do you think of these?"

"They seem to be sporadic incidences – maybe out of personal enmity – except for the Kerala massacre and the sea side blasts."

"Exactly – in the first glance, they look sporadic – but if you look closely – they seem to be connected. The main thing is there are no clues left. Nobody knows who did this – and every killing seems to be well organized and well calculated. You may be right in your say that these are sporadic – but if they are organized, then we are looking at a potential organization - we don't know anything about – and they could turn out to be dangerous to the nation."

"Do you think they are connected?"

"The first look suggests – they aren't – but you never know. What I expect from you is – use your network and investigate at your end and confirm that these are sporadic.

That will relieve me. I bank on you more than any other journalist because you have a network, you are thoroughly patriotic and you are trustworthy."

"Thank you for the compliment Sir – I will definitely try my best to see if these are connected by any chance."

"One more thing – this has to be extremely confidential – no leakages to your media. Whatever finance you need for this will be made available to you. This could be a dangerous mission because these people seem to be professional but unknown – need any protection?"

"Not as of now – if required – I will definitely ask for it."

"One more thing – we checked out Chaitanya – your new cameraman – he is trustworthy. Try and involve him in your work – the media house has already teamed him up with you. We have checked him out – he is trained in martial arts during his college days and knows to use it. His first passion was to join the Indian Army but somehow he couldn't make it to the army, though I wonder why..."

"Ok – I'll keep it in mind. Anyways – it's good to have a strongman accompany me in this mission. A person I have had a few outings with – he is a bit crazy and loves dangerous situations – he was lucky that a bullet didn't find him at Rajasthan shootout."

"If you want – take a leave and get this investigated your way – you have a good network of informers – I will cover salaries for both of you."

"Let me think – I can ask for security later if I feel so. If you say Chaitanya is good – he can take care of my security. Two questions why did you choose me? And secondly can I take this file with me?"

"They would not dream of a journalist investigating this case for us. No dear – this file is confidential; I can't let it out of this office. You can memorize the details – take as much time as you want. I fear they may have planted someone in this office as well... When you get back to office – this is what you will say and report." he pushed another file towards her.

She walked out of that office thinking all the way about what was told to her and what was noted in the confidential file...

CHAPTER EIGHT

EIGHT

Chaitanya was bored covering the press conference.

Disinterestedly, he looked around at the crowd of journalists and reporters who were covering the press conference. They were in all sizes, shapes and either supported the ruling party at the centre or against it. He could see nobody who was unbiased.

One such reporter was Bhavesh Kumar. He was asking questions that supported the cause of this leader from opposition. He was a senior journalist and was known for his hatred for the Prime Minister. He had an agenda of his own.

There was one more such journalist sitting at the other corner of the room – Dilip Desai. He was famous for his anti-Prime Minister stance and left no stone unturned to defame him. Why, he even used to manufacture news that wasn't there to suit his propaganda. Fake news was his forte...

Then there was a female journalist – Varsha Bisht. She was a supporter of Leftist and Communists. Under her garb of liberal journalistic views, she used to put every ruling and opposition party leader in trouble and she believed in talking against the Nation which she believed was bold and true journalism. She also used to manufacture news that wasn't and run her propaganda.

Anjali Verma, Lavlina Nair, Amit Kumar, Salma Shaikh, etc. – these were reporters and journalists who supported the ruling party – no matter whatever the issue – they supported them blindly. They were widely accepted by the public because they spoke well about India – there was no negative news about Prime Minister that they broadcasted. They always focused on good things by the government and if they have to speak any negative – they would normally target Pakistan and China or the opposition...

Chaitanya had not much to do – he had set his camera to the stage and was simply standing by it. He was watching all these so called journalists yap and wondered how they had managed to take sides rather than taking the side of Indian citizens. He was wondering what Priya must be doing sitting inside the office. He was now used to her type of reporting. Perhaps she was making and recording a report on the shootout at Rajasthan.

He reached the office after the press conference and looked for Priya – she wasn't there. Somebody informed him that she had a call from some government office and had to proceed there. He entered the office cafeteria and sipped on tea waiting for Priya to show up. His phone buzzed and he looked in surprise – it was Priya and she called him to his residential flat. The time for his duty was almost over so he travelled and reached home.

He called up Priya and she said that she would be there in few minutes. He started to brew coffee for them thinking why would Priya call him at his flat and not say anything on phone. The doorbell rang. It was Priya and she entered in a hurry, a bit queer for him. He looked at her with asking expression – what?

She sat down as he served the coffee brewed for both of them. Priya sipped it and sighed at the knowledge that something important had struck her...

"Chaits," that's what she called him for short, "are you willing to be on a dangerous mission?"

He was not sure what she was saying, "You know I am thirsty for some action – covering these press conferences type of events is boring."

"Are you sure that if the going gets tough you'll not back out?"

"What do you mean?"

"I mean if it's dangerous enough to put your life at stake will you back out?"

"If it's for the country or your or my life – I will not back out – I will face it head on – why are you asking thus? Are you in any sort of danger?"

"Not now – neither I nor you are into any sort of danger as of now – but maybe – we might face some danger at a later stage. I met Mr Mahal, the chief of Internal Security and IB. He has something that he wants us to do and that's going to be a top secret – you ready?"

"Ya – I am ready..." he could sense some kind of thrilling assignment and was excited at the thought 'Ah! Some action at last...'

"Listen – you and me – we are going to be a team for next couple of months or so. We will have to work closely and investigate..." she related the happenings all around the country to him, "do you think that these all are connected and pulled by some well-organized group?"

He thought for a moment, "I think these are sporadic incidences. There's a remote chance that these are connected and pulled by an organized group. But if these are pulled in by an organized group – this is dangerous – they are spread all over India and the coordination seems fantastic. It's difficult for any group to pull these attacks and remain unknown for such a long time..."

"Exactly... It's for us to find out if these are connected or just sporadic. If these are indeed sporadic, then we will not be in danger – but if they are organized and they come to know that we are investigating them – there is a chance that we will be in grave danger – so I was asking your readiness again and again..."

"Let's get the investigation done..." he said decisively, "first of all, let's find out what is common in these incidences. Then, who and why they were killed."

"How do you find out?"

"Use your network and get information about these people who were killed."

"Good idea..."

CHAPTER NINE

NINE

Priya left his flat and proceeded toward her flat. He thought of what Priya had told him – all those murders and if they were connected. Absentmindedly he ate his dinner and was still thinking and about to take rest for the night – his phone buzzed... It was Priya...

"Had your dinner?"

"Yep – what about you?"

"Yes... hey listen... Can you come over and pick me up? Something important has come up... I need your help – and anyways – now onward you are my partner in reporting..."

"Now, at 11PM? – okay... I'll take about 30 minutes to reach your place..." wondering what's come up that she wanted him urgently; he heaved himself from the bed and got ready to move. He rode at speed as the traffic on the roads by now had started to dwindle. She was waiting in the lobby of her society even as he pulled up.

"Motorcycle?" she asked looking at it in dismay, "I thought you would get a car."

"You didn't specify anything – so to reach here quickly I chose motorcycle – what's the plan?"

"We got to leave now – have to go to Karnal – there's a Mayur Dhaba in Sect 14 – we got to reach there and fast..."

"Karnal at this hour? Why?"

"You will know once we reach Karnal – don't waste time – let's go."

They rode off and were making a good speed. They halted at a pump for filling in the petrol. In about 2 hours they reached the designated dhaba. The dhaba was scantily occupied by travellers – mostly truck drivers and many night-run buses that stopped there as well. They ordered for some tea and snacks as travellers would and waited, she told him that one of her informers was going to meet her there.

There were two buses that arrived at the same time and the dhaba ran chock full even at that time of night. There was no place to sit for all the passengers. A lean man approached their table and requested a seat so that he could have his food. She waived the lean man to sit next to Chaitanya. He put his travelling sack on the table and dropped a USB next to it. Priya quickly gathered the same and put it in her purse feigning to look for something inside.

The waiter came up with their bill which they paid and left the dhaba. They stood near the motorcycle and he lit up a cigarette to while some time.

"I didn't know you smoke," she remarked, "but it's good that you do – that will act as a cover and not let anyone know why we are here. Everyone will think we are travelling back to Delhi and are waiting for you to finish off your smoke before we ride..."

"I don't smoke – but, sometimes – Yes, I do – especially, when I want to while some time without any valuable reason." he looked at her, "Why do you want to while your time – we got what we wanted – we could have been on our way."

"This is because I don't want to blow up his cover as my informer and make it seem like we don't know each other – he asked for a table to sit – I permitted him – now I am with my co-traveller waiting for him to finish his smoke before we start our travel..."

"Oh! I see..." first lesson to deal with informers and they laughed.

To a third person they seemed like a couple who were travelling and had halted for some snacks and a smoke. Once he finished his smoke, he kicked his bike revving the engine – she was about to sit on the bike as a pillion rider when they saw a bike ride into the dhaba. The riders had covered their face with towels which looked odd. They were wondering who they could be and were waiting for them to take their towels off. The buses were ready to move and the passengers were asked to take their seats. The passengers were going toward the bus. Suddenly they heard gunshots. They ran to the location to see their informer was shot dead. They looked around and saw the men whose face was covered with towels take off on their bike.

"Let's follow them..." he said and they ran back to their bike. He kicked it and revved the engine – she was on the pillion seat in a flash. They started on the road taken by those killers. They were driving fast and hazardous to catch those killers. Soon they were able to sight them and followed them. The killers sighted them and noticed that they were being followed. They shot at them and increased the speed of the bike. The bullets whizzed past Chaitanya and Priya – but they were unperturbed. These people are dangerous and both were now in their patriotic mode...

The bikes were being dangerously driven with an occasional shot from the killers. The killers turned desperately onto a desolate road. Chaitanya wanted to follow them but had to halt as a couple of trucks crossed them on the highway. He again speeded up and started following them. At one point they came to a halt as road blocks put by the police loomed up and they were waiving at them to stop.

"Stop! Stop!" a policeman shouted.

"We are following them – they just shot down a man." Chaitanya tried to reason with the policeman.

"Are you from Police?"

"No..." Priya said removing her helmet and the policeman recognized her.

"You should leave these matters to police. Hey! You are that reporter from a channel right," he recognized that she was a press reporter but couldn't remember her name or the channel – them suddenly he remembered, "You are Priya Singhal, right?"

She showed him her press id card to confirm, "Listen, why didn't you stop the motorcycle speeding on this road a few minutes ago?"

"Before we could realize, the motorcycle came to the post and sped up again – we cannot leave this barricade and alerted our HQ about a speeding motorcycle with two people."

"Did you see their face?"

"Madam - you are not in authority to question me like this – if those people have shot someone – you should be writing an FIR, not following them..."

Chaitanya looked at desolate road and knew they had lost the trail of those killers who would not only have gained distance but also made some turn and it was pointless following them.

"We seem to have lost them – can you write an FIR?"

"Here at the barricade? You must be out of your mind. You will have to go to a police station and fill in the FIR. Where did this happen?"

"At Mayur Dhaba, Karnal."

"Then you have to go to Sect 14 Karnal police station – this will not come under our jurisdiction. Go back to Karnal and find a police station nearby to that dhaba and file your FIR there..."

Despondently he looked at Priya who just shrugged her shoulders and they made way back to Karnal, found a police station and filed a FIR against unknown persons. Instead they were interrogated as to why they were out at the dead of the night. To which Priya lied that they had a wedding at Karnal and were returning to Delhi and had stopped at the dhaba for snacks when this happened. They were off on their way back to Delhi. They reached Delhi at wee hours as he dropped her off at her apartment.

"Come over to my flat and we'll see what's in the USB..."

"Dear – it's almost morning and we have not slept for the night and I have been driving almost 300 kms. Can't we see that USB tomorrow. As it goes, we have an off tomorrow – I mean today. Sleepy brain Vs Active brain after a good sleep – what would you prefer?"

She laughed at the simple way he put it, "Good night."

Next day – almost about noon, Chaitanya woke up and was lazing around with a cup of tea when his doorbell rang. He looked at the door wondering who it might be uncalled... Priya was at the door ringing the bell.

"Get up you lazy bum – she said we got work to do." she said entering into his flat.

"How come you are so early?"

"I couldn't sleep well. They killed one of my informers – the data in the USB must be important enough for them to kill him. Gimme your laptop and while I turn it on – get ready – you are in a mess..."

He freshened up and got ready to move if need be and sat next to her as she attached the USB to the laptop. Her phone buzzed. It was a landline unknown number.

"Am I speaking to Ms Priya Singhal?"

"Yes you are."

"I want to talk about the person who was killed at Karnal yesterday..." she realised that she may be receiving information about who killed the informer and put the phone on speaker mode, "I heard you were at Karnal yesterday night... and you filed a FIR for that murder."

"Yes – I did. It is imperative for a good citizen of this country to do so..."

"Did you interact with the person who was killed?"

"Why are you asking these questions – who are you?"

"Forget who I am – if you have interacted with the guy and he has provided you some information – better kept that information to yourself and if he has given you any data – destroy it – this is for your health's sake. I won't repeat – if you want to live long, healthy and lead a nice comfortable life as you are doing now – heed my words. Forget about that guy and you ever met him..." and the caller disconnected the phone.

"That was a threat call..." Chaitanya observed – "someone must be really desperate to keep hush-hush about something."

"Let's see what is in the USB and then decide..." she opened the folder in the USB and out popped a presentation – it was a presentation and 'Tool Kit' to one of the opposition parties as to how they could win the forthcoming elections. They started to run through every slide trying to understand what could be so important...

The presentation talked about how to divide the people by various methods. Chaitanya took a calculator and started calculating...

Total population – 1400000000

Gender Division by 2 – 700000000

Divide by age group of person 4 - 175000000

Divided by official languages 25 - 7000000

Divided by official dialects - 2333.333333

Divided by Primary Religions - 333.3333333

Divided by Castes / Sub Castes - 0.222222222 and so on ...

Chaitanya started laughing, "If I have to go by these calculations of Divide and Rule – **I am not even One Complete Indian...**"

"Shhh – don't joke – let's read further..."

The slides further down told how to divide the population. It also had a 'Tool Kit' of how to create clashes amongst groups of people and when and how they should be carried out. The groups will clash – religion to religion, caste to caste and create mayhem in the country... It also identified criminals who would do that, where and how much they would charge to get it done. Where and how the arson was to be carried out... Once the mayhem begins how should the leaders of this opposition party approach the masses and how they should blame the current Prime Minister for it... also the usage of social media – facebook, twitter, YouTube, etc and who would run a propaganda, run disruptive content and make the party look sensible, thus creating inroads in the minds of people that these leaders know the pulse of the people and how they are the ones who should lead the country... and not the current Prime Minister.

"This is a dangerous plan. Lot of people will be affected. This also has a plan to stop the nation from growing with clashes and arson. This has to be stopped. What if we tell this on TV and inform people not to fall for such provocations?"

"Will not work – they will say that this is an agenda against their party – and you know many journalists are biased and take sides to defame parties. Secondly, this is a plan for one opposition party – we don't know what other parties are planning including the ruling party – telling this to people on TV will only warn these parties in advance and they will be more discreet. It will be tough then to get any informer to steal their plan and let anyone know..."

"What is the plan then? – we cannot sit quiet on this piece of information – too dangerous for the nation."

She made a copy of that presentation and kept the USB in his shirt pocket and dialled a number. She spoke to the person and said, "Let's go out for lunch. Let's go to Bukhara and have a filling lunch that deserves a holiday mood."

CHAPTER TEN

TEN

Priya started toward the door – Chaitanya blocked it...

"Bukhara! Are you out of your head – it's costly. Can't we go to some other affordable place?"

"Don't worry about the cost – the bill is on me – you simply accompany me..."

"Ok – let's go – we will take the bike – car will get stuck in the traffic..." and they left for the venue.

They reached Bukhara. She entered the place while he found a place to park and followed her. The place was full during the lunch time and they had to wait till one of the tables was vacant. Priya and Chaitanya occupied their seats and were about to order when she suddenly got up excited, "Mr Das – remember me – I am Priya Singhal, reporter. Nice to see you visit a normal restaurant like this..." she smiled at him.

He smiled back and said "Yes dear I do remember you and your tough interview that had me sweating..." and he winked as she laughed at the memory, "I guess, I will have to wait for a table – the place seems to be full."

"Oh! Why don't you join us – promise – no questions – just light hearted talks and the lunch..." she proposed to Mr Das.

"Not a bad idea – I will join you – and there are 2 more people with me – even they will join you..." he beckoned to a couple, “Meet her – she is Simran, my secretary and he is Maj. Nair, my security in chief...”

“Oh! Hello to both of you – and he is Chaitanya – my colleague and uses his camera abilities to my report’s advantage...”

After a round of Hi’s and Hello’s they settled down and ordered for their lunch. Priya bent over and whispered to Chaitanya that Mr Das was a big officer in IB and this was the plan to collect that USB – this lunch was a setup as cover up of this operation. They all ate with appetite and their stomachs were full after a hearty meal.

Chaitanya got up, “Excuse me, I will have to go to the washroom – my bowels seem to be full.”

“That reminds me, even my bowels are full, I will join you.” Mr Das said and they crossed over to the washroom followed by Maj. Nair. They entered the washroom and was secured to be empty and safe, Maj. Nair stepped out and stood on to secure entry to the washroom, “where’s the data Priya told me about – you have it on you or Priya has it in her custody?”

Chaitanya was a bit dazzled by all the occurrences – this was the first time he was dealing with IB officer and acting like a spy. He pulled out the USB from his pocket and handed it over to Mr Das, who in response gave him a thick packet, “give this packet to Priya...” and they returned to the table. Mr Das insisted that he pays the bill, paid it and left with his secretary and Maj. Nair.

“Do you have a smoke on you?” Priya asked him.

“I didn’t know you smoke too...”

“Idiot – the smoke is for you to while away some time so that anyone looking thinks it was by chance that we met Mr Das.”

He quietly lit up a smoke and clicked her photos as if she wanted to post them on her social media accounts and she was giving directions as to how she wanted the photos to be... They looked like a normal pair of friends or a couple posing in front of the restaurant for their memories and posts on the Instagram.

"Ok – this is it – today's work is over. Let's go to my flat. I will brew a coffee for us..." she said and hopped on behind him – on the way they filled in petrol – the tank was almost empty with the drive to Karnal and back from that chase.

"Oh! Wow! – you have quite a decent flat that you have rented..." he said as he entered the flat – the interiors seem to be quite good.

"Ambience – you know..." she said with a mock attitude and walked into the kitchen to brew the coffee.

"Hey - not so much – but I would like my flat done a bit better," he said sipping the coffee, "if you could help me arrange it to be better, I would be delighted."

"Anytime you want the makeover dude..." she assured him. After sipping the coffee, he got up to go over to his flat. She came along with him as she wanted to buy few groceries. They said bye and he went to the parking lot to get his bike while she started walking towards the main gate of the society. He pulled his bike out of the parking lot and kicked it started to ride it toward his flat.

He reached outside the main gate and checked if Priya was in sight – to his horror, he saw an old Maruti van stop by her. He saw tough men get out of the car and push her into it and abduct her. He raced behind the van to save Priya from her abductors. The van had covered some distance between them and he had to almost stand on his bike time to time to watch where it was heading. They were heading towards the Meerut road. He kept following trying to get close to the van – but the traffic didn't allow him to get closer.

Soon the van made its way to the highway and picked up speed. He had a tough time in keeping up with the speed of the van. The toll plaza there made them stop for a while and he was able to sight them again. He wished they would have stopped for a little longer – he would have rescued her then and there. Again on the highway, he knew that it would be tough to follow their speed. He sped his bike behind them for some distance when the van veered onto a smaller road and he followed.

Soon the van entered into an old bungalow in the outskirts of Bana. The space around was open and he couldn't risk being seen approach the bungalow. It was almost evening and nearing the sunset. He parked his bike about half a furlong away by a road side stall that was closed. He started making it on foot trying to judge how many men he would have to tackle in the process...

Inside the bungalow – Priya was taken to a dark room and made to sit in a chair while her hands were securely tied behind the chair. Suddenly a focus lamp shown on her making her bink, she could see some shadows of about 5 people in the room. They were silent – none spoke a word – they were simply standing still. The door to the room opened showing some light behind and a man walked in – he seemed more sinister and downright dangerous... He sat in front of her – she couldn't see his face.

"So – Miss Priya Singhal – that's your name, right? What were you doing at Karnal yesterday at that time of night?"

She just looked on saying nothing and he kept waiting for her answer...

"I repeat – what were you doing in Karnal last night?"

"I had gone there to attend the wedding of my friend and was returning with one of my friends..."

"You are a good liar Miss Priya ... again ... what were you doing in Karnal last night?"

"I told you the truth..." she realized that these men were someone from those who had killed her informer and wanted to know what he had informed her...

"You realize that if we can kill that rat – you are an easy target to kill..."

"Why kill me for something I don't know about..." she was buying some time hoping that Chaitanya had seen these people abduct her and would do something to help her, "I don't know the person who was killed – I don't know you and I don't want to know. You are following up a wrong lead. Let me go and I will not tell what happened here or that you abducted me..."

"Nice try – once again – what were you doing at Karnal yesterday? We saw him sit on your table and have his food – did he pass any information to you while he was eating his meal?"

"There was no place at the dhaba and the poor guy wanted to eat a meal – he requested if he could share the table and we permitted. That's all to what you are asking – nothing more. Next when my friend was smoking in the parking we heard gunshots and find that person killed..."

"Hmm – a tough nut to crack I guess – you will not tell us so easily – I am thinking of ways to torture you into telling us the truth..."

She realized that these people meant business and will stop at nothing. The data had a plan so dangerous to the nation that millions of people will be affected if it was implemented by these people. She braced herself for torture – nation comes first... her life didn't mean much in comparison to the nation...

"Ok – let's ask you another question – why did you follow the people who shot that rat?"

"It was my friend's idea – he wanted a thrill in his life – so he followed them. I was with him on his bike so I had to be with him – cannot be at the dhaba all by myself at night..." she tried veering the topic off and buying more time.

"I think you won't answer till we start torturing you – Chhotu, what kind of torture do you think would be best for her?"

She could sense Chhotu's lust...

"She is a sexy babe." Chhotu began, "and it is dangerous for our plan to be leaked. I am sure she has some or all the information. Why don't we keep her here for a life time? – she can be used for our enjoyment when we need it."

"But, you realize – we are not here all the time..."

"Let's remove her clothes off and burn them – she wouldn't dare to escape nude. It'll not be good for her dashing news reporter image – people will look at her as someone who was found nude and that will hamper her image. She won't be able to show her face to anyone again – her own fraternity of media will want to show her in nude state for want of TRP – if she does happen to escape in nude condition. Further – it will be easy for us to enjoy her body whenever we want to – no complicated dress to remove..." he proposed with a vicious laughter that echoed in the room - more in her mind. She just hoped that Chaitanya had seen these people abducting her and was getting help.

"Good idea Chhotu – I would like you to see the delicacy of your hands as you remove her blouse – unbuttoning it – one by one..." his attention turned toward Priya again as Chhotu in the shadows of darkness, walked slowly with deliberateness and stood behind her, "Now – darling – please tell me the truth. I promise it would be a simple bullet through your head with no nonsense or a life full of rape..."

Priya could sense that these people were truly dangerous and will do anything to get the information from her. She knew that the information was important and had a dangerous plan that would disrupt the country – she would not let some people hold her nation ransom for greed of power. She braced for whatever was to come – her heart sinking that Chaitanya had not seen these men abduct her...

"Courageous men are you – torturing a girl with hands tied behind and nobody to protect her – kudos to your courage..." she jeered them with a hope that at least one of the men present there would be hurt with her words and take her side... but she was wrong.

"Chhotu – begin your job..." and Chhotu slowly unbuttoned the top button of her collared neck blouse... and stopped.

"One down – few more to go – tell me the truth..." she just looked at him in anger and hate, "Chhotu – one more..." and Chhotu gently opened the second button of her blouse and stopped there, "Darling if you want to sleep with us – just say so – why arouse us in such a fashion... The truth..."

"You people deserve death – you are not humans – you are devils – my curse will fall upon you and you'll all die..." she said in her anger and in her anguish to which the people in the room laughed. Chhotu opened up the third button of her blouse clearly showing the cleavage of her breasts.

"You still have a chance to tell the truth and die honourably – unless you are that type of a girl who wants to be naughty..."

Chhotu was about to touch her breasts when the door opened and a couple of men entered. Without warning they shot the people in the room with their silencer fitted guns – and made sure that those people were dead. A sound of a soft whistle sounded and they left as they had arrived on scene – silently. Chaitanya entered the room within a minute... he looked at Priya aghast...

"Are you alright?" he asked untying her, "What happened here?" – he looked around and found a switch to illuminate the room. He looked in disbelief at the dead bodies of men around.

"They were going to rape me..." she said with her expression blank. Chaitanya realized that she was in some kind of trauma and looked around – quickly gathered her purse and her mobile. He clicked the photos of dead men for reference. He looked around to see if any other giveaway signs that she was here in the room and found nothing. He buttoned up her blouse for her and had to drag her out of that bungalow. He knew that she would take some time to get over her trauma and didn't ask more questions. Fortunately, the road was deserted and he was able to drag her to the place where he had parked his bike. He rode to her flat with her clinging behind in terror of what had happened.

CHAPTER ELEVEN

ELEVEN

Priya was still in trauma and he had to search her purse to find the key to her flat. He knew telling police will only raise doubts about what they were up to – he picked up her phone and dialled the last number – it belonged to Mr Das. He was shocked to hear of entire event and said not to worry – he was sending a military doctor immediately to her flat to take care of medication and her traumatic feeling. He said that he will arrange security for her and asked him to stay with her till doctor arrived.

He ordered for food for both of them and somehow managed to feed her in the condition that she was... and had a small wait till the military doctor showed up. The doctor gave her a soothing shot and prescribed some traumatic medicines for her and kept her company till he got the medicines form a nearby stores. The doctor advised him to say anything that would pep her up and give her confidence to be herself again and left.

She was feeling sleepy after the soothing injection and she looked at Chaitanya who with care had fed her food and was now giving her the pills.

"Don't go..." she said, "I'm scared they will return and I don't want to be alone when they come for me..." she pleaded, "I have two beds in the bedroom, one for any relatives who visit me – you can sleep there – that way I will be assured that you are with me and I am safe..." he smiled at her and yielded. He knew that Mr Das must have made arrangement for her security but he couldn't leave her in that traumatic condition. He put her to sleep and spread on the bed meant for her relatives.

He was thinking about how dangerous was the plot and how desperate was the party that was planning such a lowly game to quench their thirst for power and forget the national interest. The slides of that presentation were zooming around in his mind and he was trying to fit some pieces together. He fell asleep... somewhere deep in the night, he felt weight on his shoulder and on his chest. He looked around to see Priya who had got out of her bed and was clinging on to him, "I am scared..." she said, to which he simply patted her head as a reassurance that he was with her and she slept soundly.

He woke up and found her still sleeping on his bed, almost clinging to him. He gently freed himself and freshened up – entered her kitchen and prepared tea. He returned to the bedroom and saw her sleeping peacefully and went to the hall and put on the TV. There was no news of what had happened to Priya yesterday or about the people killed in the bungalow. I think either the police have not found them or the media was still not informed about any incidence...

There was a strange cry from her and he rushed back to the bedroom. She looked terrified and held him tight. She had not come out of her trauma. She was scared to be alone, even inside her bedroom. He asked her to freshen up while he brewed her tea and prepared a breakfast of clumsy omelettes. She felt a bit better after that and sat in the hall with him. He deliberately put on a cartoon channel for her to watch.

"You watch cartoons – at this age?" she asked a bit confused.

"I think – cartoons are the best way to lighten up the mood and forget all the trouble for some time – age doesn't matter..." and she started to watch cartoons along with him – reliving the days of her childhood.

The doctor religiously visited and checked Priya for any deep sign of trauma – he was relieved she was not so much in trauma and decided that she would be out of it within a week. Only that Chaitanya has to keep pepping her and boosting her confidence.

"I have to go and get my stuff if I have to stay here..." he told her truthfully and she again panicked – then it was decided that she will come with him to his flat and stay there because whoever abducted her knew this place she had rented and could come for her again. So she picked up her stuff and got ready to move into his flat. They rented a cab as she wasn't comfortable to ride with him on his bike – those people could see her get out of her flat and follow them. Chaitanya shook his head to see her in this condition and yielded.

They reached his flat and settled there. He had to order another bed for her in urgency. He didn't own a TV and he felt that was good – he didn't want Priya to see news or hear news – he wanted her to become normal again.

When she was sleeping, he copied the number of Mr Das and dialled him to ask if he was able to find any information about the group who had abducted Priya. He said that they were working on the matter and soon they will be apprehended. He asked if Chaitanya knew who had killed those abductors – he hadn't seen any dead bodies around and said he will have to wait till Priya gets well – she must have seen those people.

Mr Das informed him that they had to identify the gang of goons and their main leader – the don and they were collecting any evidence they could get to nab and put them in judicial custody till Priya got well – that was more important. He said that he had gone through the 'Tool Kit' and had identified the people who were going to create trouble along with few leaders who were responsible. He would be able to take some action on them and round them up in about few days. He asked him to be careful and alert till then...

With nothing to do, he called up his office and informed them that he and Priya had met with a small accident and will be out of action for a week. He browsed his mobile for some information on the massacre of those abductors – but nobody had any news. Mr Das called him to ask if he could identify any of the abductors to which he sent the photos of the dead abductors to him. Even he was nonplussed about who could have helped Priya and killed those goons.

The entire week saw Priya almost sleeping all the while, waking up for lunch or dinner and for few minutes intermittently when they played simple games like Ludo, snakes and ladders, etc. He was trying to make her as comfortable as possible. They were discussing possibilities of renting a bigger flat with more bedrooms and sharing that flat so that they could be together all the while and at a new place which will mean it will be difficult for anybody to locate her easily.

He kept in touch with the studio and his colleagues keeping Priya away from them telling that she was recovering and its best she is left alone to rest than getting excited with daily hustle bustle...

In the meantime – he kept asking his colleagues and the other reporters what the news was – he was a bit in doubt as to why the news of the massacre at the bungalow was not known to anybody... who was keeping the news from spreading and why...

He also was speaking to Priya and telling her how brave she was and how she should get up and fight the entire system. How she could be instrumental in saving the nation. He cited the example that these kind of big sharks who even the law had to think twice before apprehending were treating her as an enemy and how important was her work to the nation... she kept listening to his pep talk and gaining confidence. She also knew that if he was with her 24 hours – she would feel safe to carry out what he was saying – a service to the nation which was necessary and would save lots of lives, property and bring the criminals to justice.

CHAPTER TWELVE

TWELVE

While Priya was recovering from her trauma – something else was going on – the stage was set – Mr Das had started to make arrangements to apprehend those involved in the 'Tool Kit' and those who would be involved in nefarious activities later on...

He had given all the names in the 'Tool Kit' to his associates and asked everybody to search out even the miniscule offence by them – so that they can be apprehended under that garb and then they would be grilled to tell the truth. Saving the nation from internal clashes of huge masses was something that was more important. His team was working on it – he had planned to apprehend them, all at the same time with a single sweep of action...

Varsha Bisht was in Amritsar trying to justify the movement of Khalistanis. She had an exclusive interview with Ajaypal Singh who was a prime face of the movement. He had said a lot in that interview and she had subtly supported him and his views. She was already drawing a lot of flak for the interview and her anti-national stance from the public. Someone was paying her good for this work... her name was in 'Tool Kit' as one of the propaganda head...

She again met Ajaypal Singh for another interview for her YouTube channel and had returned to her hotel room.

She was sitting and editing the video so that it looked more as government's failure rather than a madman trying to be popular and carrying on with the agenda of Pakistan. She ordered for a cup of tea and someone knocked the door. She saw a lady in burkha at the door and realized that she must have brought her payment. Instead the lady in burkha removed a silencer fitted gun and shot her dead.

She was found by one of the hotel staff who had brought in the tea and was rushed to a nearby hospital – and was declared dead on arrival. The media was in frenzy that this had happened to a fellow reporter – they had forgotten for the time being that she was in a camp of reporters and journalists who spoke against the nation...

Slowly the news of other members listed in the 'Tool Kit' started to trickle in – they were being killed one by one and in a manner that left no trace behind. Even the smaller leaders around the country were a target and were being killed. All in all – the mayhem had begun – but not for the nation – it had begun for the party who had plotted against the nation...

Chaitanya was happy that this was happening and that Priya would now be safe to move out again – he had the doubt that the 'Tool Kit' had something to do with her abduction. He had identified each and every person in the 'Tool Kit' using his sources and the internet and was crossing them out in dead man's folder as and when their death was being reported. He could sense the tension that the main leaders of that party could be going through – looking and digesting everyone they had banked on were being killed. He was sure that Mr Das had arranged all these killings through Special Forces of IB...

It was after 5 days that she dared to get out of that flat with Chaitanya – as decided they had to look for a bigger flat which would accommodate both of them comfortably. She was now feeling much confident which was visible as they searched a flat and finalised it. They left the cab at her old accommodation where she picked up more clothes and they rode back to his flat on his bike which was parked in her society.

"Chaits – what's happening in the world?"

"Seems – you are ready and raring to go out and do what you have to do for the nation..."

"Thanks to your care and your pep talk – I am alright and out of the fear that I felt after that episode – do you have the updates?"

"The update is – I am not sure if it was for the informer who was killed in Karnal or the 'Tool Kit' that landed in you in trouble..."

"It was both – the informer who was killed at Karnal and the USB of the 'Tool Kit' – they seemed to know I had the information..." she interrupted him...

"So – I was saying that the update is – whosoever was listed in the 'Tool Kit' and their goons are on the run – it seems Mr Das has assigned the task to Special Forces and they are hunting these guys and killing them – making the way smoother for you."

"Really – I should thank Mr Das for it..." and she dialled his number. Strangely, Mr Das asked her to come to IB office to meet him and Mr Mahal. She was a bit confused as to why she was being called to their office. She decided to check it out and asked Chaitanya to come along with her – she still was not sure of her safety...

Chaitanya and Priya sat in the reception of the IB and were ushered in after a wait of 20-30 minutes. Mr Mahal was sitting at his desk and Mr Das was sitting on the sofa chair that faced Priya and Chaitanya...

"Welcome, my girl, how are you doing?" Mr Mahal said as they took their places on the chairs facing him.

"As of now – okay – but I am still not sure of my safety."

"That's what I have called you to tell me – I heard you were abducted and Chaitanya here rescued you from them. Tell me what exactly happened... do not keep anything from me – knowing that is most important to me..."

She started relating it from the point of her abduction, how she was put in the van, how mean looking man pulled a gun on her so that she comes along quietly – then how she was dragged and tied to the chair and what questions they asked and how they were thinking of torturing her (here she was a bit scared as well angry about their behaviour) and then how suddenly 2 men appeared on the scene and shot all the bad men and left on a soft whistle – and then Chaitanya appeared on the scene...

Mr Mahal looked at Mr Das and thought for a while, "Do you remember anyone's face – did you recognize anybody there?"

"Nopes – I didn't see their faces as they were sitting in the dark with light flashing on my face – however I will recognize the faces of men in the car who abducted me..."

"Even I didn't see anyone around – when I found her – she was tied to a chair with dead people around her." Chaitanya said pulling out his mobile, "I clicked some pictures of dead men – perhaps you could recognize them..." he said helpfully.

She looked at the pictures and recognized one of them to be her abductor – the rest she didn't know who they were...

"Hmm – it seems there is a third party involved in this – they could be their rivals or goons from some other party who want to play the dirty game differently."

"I didn't understand." Both of them said in unison.

“Listen – our plan was to incriminate them and by weekend arrest all of them under some pretext so that we could interrogate them...” Mr Das started to explain, “Someone is on a killing spree and has decided to kill them all. About 70% of the names in that ‘Tool Kit’ you got – are killed – and it’s not us. Nor any Special Forces of the government or the police... who could it be?”

Priya and Chaitanya looked blankly at Mr Das for this information, they had presumed it was Mr Das and IB’s Special Forces were killing the people named in the ‘Tool Kit’.

“Can I see the photographs you clicked of the dead people at the bungalow – we didn’t find any corpses there...” Chaitanya handed his phone over to Mr Das who copied the photographs in his laptop and from there in to a USB. He stepped outside for a minute before returning to his seat.

“So – it wasn’t IB or any of government’s Special Forces who are killing these people...” Chaitanya made a statement.

‘Exactly... And we would like to know who...” Mr Mahal pulled out 2 pieces of papers, neatly laminated, and handed them over to Priya and Chaitanya, “These are licenses for keeping guns – just for safety – but a legal necessity. Next month, you will attend the training of how to use guns – this is for your safety – the things are getting uglier by the day and you seemed to be marked by these people – I think you are closer to solving the mystery of these murders than you think...”

“We have no clue as to what’s going on...”Priya was not ready to believe what Mr Mahal had said, “We don’t know who is killing these men in Delhi and elsewhere...”

“Correct – but, those people seem to think so...” Mr Mahal stopped as Mr Das’s phone buzzed. He waited till his conversation was over and raised an eyebrow...

"You were right Mr Mahal – nobody found bodies at the bungalow – because whoever killed those men – took the bodies and threw them around in fields spread over 200 km area. Thus there was no uproar and everyone thought that these were separate incidences..."

"See where I am coming to – Priya – keep your eyes and ears open and use your links and informers to get any information you can on them – all the best and stay safe. Don't forget your training on guns..." Mr Mahal was a bit concerned about her safety.

"I wouldn't dream of killing a person with a gun." Chaitanya said and Priya nodded - exactly that's what she wanted to say.

"No need to kill – but you can very well scare those people away if you are in trouble..." Mr Mahal advised and they left his office thinking about what they had gotten into...

CHAPTER THIRTEEN

THIRTEEN

"Hey – let's start from the beginning – that will help us relate the events clearly. We went to Karnal. You allowed the informer to sit at our table and picked up that USB." Chaitanya was on a thought process, "Then those men on bike killed your informer and rode off. We started following them and they turned off the highway where police barricade was put up. They managed to escape the barricade and we were stuck answering the policemen. Then we came back and next day, you got a threat call..." Priya nodded that nothing was missing in the link. "I now have a doubt that either those at the barricade were not policemen but conmen attached to that party or if they indeed were policemen – then either one or all of them are corrupt and squealed that we were following those killers – else how would those people know that it was you who could have probably met the informer and got the knowledge of what was in that USB?"

"You are quite a sleuth Chaits – you should be in criminal case solving..." Priya smiled at that at least their thoughts were on proper line, "yes – I don't see any other way those goons could have known this fact. Had we returned quietly from Karnal – maybe – those goons wouldn't have any idea of this meeting."

"Now that we know, we can tell Mr Das to investigate those so called policemen. Other thing bothers me though – where are these people getting information about the 'Tool Kit' of who is named in them?"

"Beats me though..." Priya also was thinking hard, "It could be that the informer could have made 2 copies and handed one over to the people who are killing – else – someone at Mr Das's office or Mr Das himself must have leaked that information... Let's wait till we get any other information like this and check..."

They decided to wait and watch what was going on till an informer came up with some information. And one of her informers did come up with another piece of information...

"Radha Natekar – a person who ran a NGO for opposing any and every project of National interest under the garb of people safety, people displacement and environment had received a huge amount from various sources. It runs in crores of rupees..." Priya was relating what the informer had told her, "She is popular activist – mostly with the people who follow left and liberal views."

"So what – whenever I can manage I do charity work for NGOs like PRATHAM and SMILE FOUNDATION and likewise. If people donate money to such NGOs – it is for good of the Nation..."

"The twist is – her NGO has received this donation in a single day – about 15 crore rupees – and guess what these have been put by 200 various donors – all put the same amount of 750000 each... the doubt is why same amount? And the other thing is all are Ghost accounts – the people who transferred the amount are not real... Why do you think this money could have been transferred?"

“Could be for resistance to any of the latest projects government has planned – she likes opposing government for any and every development project, right?”

“Ok – that leads to us to somewhere – let’s check out which are the projects that government has planned – and then we can zero in on the project she would oppose – this will be a big expose on the media...”

“Let’s see ... There is this project in Arunachal Pradesh of about 50 small scale dams to be built to generate hydel power for various remote areas... then there is Sagarmala project which intends to build or develop various ports in India, connecting it by road and rail so that the exports can be magnified and made easy...”

“Then there is Bharatmala project which is to develop roads, highways and mega highways to connect the nation in a solid way ...” Chaitanya added, “this obviously could be her target as the land of people will be required to be acquired...”

“Then there is Inland Waterways Project which will open up inland travel using the rivers and canals. About 14-15 such rivers and canals have been identified – even this could be on the list – reason cited could be pollution of the rivers and canals...”

“So there are three projects where she can raise the objection and stall these projects – now the question is – who are the people who could put such a huge amount to fund her NGO – after all 15 crores is not a small amount...”

“It could be illegal money – what we call as black money – transferred, to convert it into white. This could be done by corrupt politicians who have access to such huge amounts or rich people outside India or anti-national elements with a tie-up with organizations who want to disturb the pace at which, we as a nation are growing... but the same amount by 200 ghost accounts is something that needs investigation..."

"She obviously will say that she doesn't know who donates the money to her NGO – it's people's will... This is our chance – let's tell Mr Das and see what happens..."

"Good idea – the expose over media can wait for 2 days – it will be interesting what Mr Das does in this case..." and they called up Mr Das to tell him the news... Mr Das assured them that he'll take the investigation further and thanked them.

"Now what we will have to wait is what does Mr Das do about it? And who she transfers the money to? Will your informer know if she transfers money to anyone?"

"Today is Friday evening – he will most probably take action on Monday – we have time to kill. What about a short trip to Nainital? – it will be a great change for us – we leave now and return on Sunday evening or Monday evening..."

"Good idea..." they packed small sacks and left for their trip. It was a welcome trip for Priya who now was able to overcome her trauma and be herself. She was the same old Priya and her photos on Instagram that Chaitanya knew and he was glad at her recovery.

They returned late on Sunday and joined the work on Monday. To keep her from going out on the field, the chief editor asked her to present the news from the newsroom as an anchor. She took over the news presenter's role for that day while Chaitanya had to go out with another anchor for reporting the strike and the dharna put by a political party against the government. When he returned, she was presenting the last piece of news in the regular bulletin and he couldn't stop laughing – she was getting distracted even if he was behind the soundproof glass wall that separated the news room...

She finished presenting the news and came out of the news room, "What's making you laugh?" she asked Chaitanya who went into another fit of laughter irritating her...

"Don't mind my laughter. Take off your heavy makeup that you put on for camera and we are ready to go. I will wait in the cafeteria for you while I sip at a cup of tea..."

After some time she joined him for tea and they left for their flat, "Was the makeup too much? Did I look horrible in that makeup?" she asked not sure of his laughter and he again had a fit of laughter...

"Let me drive – don't say a word..." Chaitanya said controlling his laughter and stayed on the road, "let's dine out – I feel like it..." he suggested and she agreed. She was dying to know what had made Chaitanya laugh so much – but didn't ask for he may spray her with something while eating and laughing. Once they reached home she asked about his laughter again.

"Were you reading out news or scaring whoever was watching it?" he couldn't hold his laughter again.

"What do you mean – I presented the news like I always do whenever the editor asks me to... what's so funny about it?"

"In about 25 minutes, they will have the recording re-telecast – and I want you to see that – you will know that you were scaring the people who would watch..."

They watched the re-telecast on the phone mobile and even she joined him in his laughter, "I have to curb the habit of frowning and using a sharp tone while presenting news..." she observed and again started to laugh. While he liked that he had heard this laughter after almost 10 days.

Her phone buzzed, it was Mr Das, "Where have you been? Ok – now listen to breaking news you will have to air tomorrow evening not before that – it's your exclusive ... Radha Natekar has been summoned by the ED in context to the ghost account investors putting more than 15 crores. A team of ED has been sent to Mumbai for investigation and she will be first interrogated and if need be taken into custody by tomorrow evening."

"Hmm – Mr Das seems to be honest – he's taking legal action against Radha Natekar." Priya said looking at Chaitanya.

"Let's see – tomorrow's another day..." was his reply.

CHAPTER FOURTEEN

FOURTEEN

Next day in the morning, NEWS telecast that Radha Natekar on her way back to Mumbai met with an accident late at night and was run over by a truck that was stolen – the person driving the truck has escaped and without a trace...

"See what I predicted – so today is another day indeed..." he said and they were now convinced that Radha Natekar was killed at the behest of Mr Das.

He set up his mobile camera at a nice corner of the flat and recorded the news which she presented deftly. Sent it to the studio while she called her editor and briefed him about the scene not sharing that Mr Das had given this information about the ED. The editor in 15 minutes got the editing done, the news presentation done and aired it on the channel. He sent a team of a local reporter and the cameraman to her residence for household member's reaction, but they weren't home. They were in the village in Maharashtra where she was planning her next protest against the government and had met with an accident.

They were summoned by the editor and reached their office. He asked how they got this information to which they said that an unknown source had called them and given this information. They had called a source in ED and they had confirmed the news.

"Good – jolly good!" The editor was happy for he was getting his TRP, "Now I want you to go to Rajasthan and cover a fascinating scene – A sign of Goodwill and Religious Tolerance being organized by the communities. The event is scheduled for day after tomorrow – but you have to be careful, there may be criminals and anti-social elements that would try and disrupt the event. You will cover the event and try and find out if any anti-social elements want to disrupt and report to me. This is at Jodhpur and you are booked at our partner hotel... Good luck and take care..."

They left the office for their flat and packed a couple of clothes for the event coverage and were on their way off to Jodhpur. It was Eid and Akshay Trutiya, which also was Parshuram Jayanti, and the crowds were enthusiastic about celebrating both the religious pious day together – it was a brotherly feeling between the two communities...

They reached 2 days before and rested for some time. Then they met the organizers who were setting of this **Example of Brotherhood** and interviewed them. It was a dream that such an event was being organized. After the interview they had not much work – so they walked in the bazaar. She entered a cloth shop that was selling traditional Rajasthani dresses. She selected one of the dresses and tried it – she asked for some alterations to the dress and was happy when the shopkeeper told her that she would get the dress altered within an hour. She then shopped for traditional ornaments and collected them. Then they collected her dress and headed to the hotel.

Next day they travelled to the venue and recorded the arrangement and the preparations. The event was supposed to be magnanimous – on one side of the main road near Jalori Gate, the Hindus would be offering prayers and with a partition installed, the other side Muslims were to offer namaz. The road looked beautiful as the Green and Saffron flags decorated both the sides. At the time of the prayer, they were supposed to lay a white cloth on the road to signify the Indian flag.

The event was supposed to start around 5PM and was supposed to follow with sweet distribution amongst all the people. Everyone was filled with enthusiasm for it was the first of its kind and was a proof of solidarity between the people of both religions towards the nation.

In the morning of the event, Priya had gone out early leaving a message on Chaitanya's number that she wanted to go the parlour to get ready and will be back by noon. He need not wait for lunch and have it when he feels hungry. In his room he checked his camera for its proper functioning and kept it charged. With nothing to do – he lazed out again. Then had his lunch and lazed out again. He sprang up as his phone buzzed. It was Priya – she was ready and it was time to go to the venue to cover the event...

He gathered his camera and quickly freshened up and moved toward her room in the hotel. She wasn't there so he called up and found that she was on the terrace of the hotel. The terrace of that hotel was beautifully adorned by a garden that bloomed pretty flowers and a great display. He looked around and she gracefully walked out from behind a pillar with huge Tea-Urn that added to the beauty of the place... He looked on stunned...

She looked stunning and absolutely out of a magazine – she wore a Kanchli and a multi-coloured Ghagra which she had bought yesterday. The dress suited her and gracefully showed off her curves. She adorned a Rajasthani traditional Odhni over her head through which her crowning glory and her beautifully done hair peeped out. On her head she wore a Rakhdi giving her face a divine look – apart from the Jhaale with Kundan or maybe Meenakari works... She wore a Tussi on her neck making her look like a queen – Baju Bandh and the Gokhrus adorned her slim and beautiful arms along with traditional colourful bangles – she also wore a Adah, a special necklace that's worn by Rajputs to add to the fervour – she was adorned with a Kardhani around the waist and a Payal on her ankle making her looks – absolutely devastating... and the Kadhani as well her Payal made sweet musical notes when she moved...

"You are ready to get married, Priya..." she laughed at this statement and moved toward him making a tinkling musical sound.

"Not so soon..." she gave a pose, "Click my pictures..."

"Instagram..." he sighed looking at the sky and shaking his head and went about clicking her photos. She must have clicked at least 50 of them before she was ready to move to the venue...

The hotel cab dropped them at the Jallori Gate's outskirts as the roads leading in were closed for the event. They walked their way to the venue. The organizers welcomed them and showed the points which were suitable for them to shoot the event. They selected one and said that they will be back for the event if this place could be reserved for their channel... The organizers agreed and put a placard of their channel to book that position for them...

This done they started shooting the arrangements – the editing will come later at the studio – they did their job – recording and reporting what they saw... they also interviewed few people of both sides who were participating and felt proud that they were Indians – True Indians...

"Let's have a tea at that stall before it gets shut for the event..." Chaitanya suggested and they went to the tea stall. The stall owner was dazzled by her beauty and didn't recognise her to be a reporter who appeared almost every day on her channel which was popular... Chaitanya looked around and saw a building under construction, close to the venue by the road and near the mosque, "Let's get on top of that construction to get a bird's eye view of the event..." and they approached the construction, saw the entrance and climbed a whole 3 floors to reach the top.

"Ugh – this place is filled with all the construction material – bricks, stones, sand – that will dirty my dress, let's go a floor below and see if that is clean..." she objected and he looked at her a bit irritated.

"You keep a stay here while I gather the bird's eye view..." she didn't say a word but stood on the landing of the steps while he walked through the construction piles to the edge and started recording the marvellous sight. He could clearly distinguish the tri-colour made by the flags and the white cloth spread at the centre... He loved the sight and shot the sight with more detail. After recording what he wanted to, he returned to the spot where Priya was and started to say something but stopped.

She put a finger to her lips signalling him to be quiet, "I think we are on to something..." she whispered, "there are men gathering on the first floor and their behaviour looks suspicious."

"Ok – let's check it out. Don't make any sound which will alert them..." and he started tiptoeing down the steps. She raised her ghagra up to her knees and followed him, making sure that her Kardhani or the Payal didn't make any sound. They reached the 2nd floor and stopped there were more people walking up the steps. They had to wait till they entered a room that was being built. He looked cautiously and made sure that nobody was coming up the steps as well nobody was on guard at the entrance or the steps. He signalled to her and they tiptoed again down to the 1st floor and made way around the hall those people had assembled. There was a small opening in the wall where he thrust his camera and started recording the faces in the crowd.

"I believe everyone is present now... Let me start to explain what we are going to do..." one of the men dressed in a pathani suit started to address the meeting, "At sharp 8PM when the prayers are over with and the sweets from both sides are to be distributed – we are going to attack the Hindu crowd. The group here will go to the terrace of this building where we have kept lots of bricks and stones – they will start pelting it down on the crowd..." by this time Chaitanya had captured all the faces in the crowd and had taken the camera off from that hole and they were able to hear the person saying this clearly.

"What about us Janab Ismail Sharif?" one of the other crowd members asked.

"Shh – nobody knows I am from ISI and am here to carry out this mission – to Indian authorities I am Ismailbhai who runs a madarsa near Jallori Gate... never take my real name..."

"Sorry Ismailbhai – please carry on..."

"Nobody knows that we are not from Jodhpur. I know that we all are assembled here for this mission. These are the leaders for groups 1 to 5 – they are our sleeper cells – they will lead you and tell you what you have to do – for groups 5-10, these are your leaders. We know you are not Indians but either are Bangladeshi or Rohingya fugitives seeking shelter in this country, the administration still has to find this out. This is the word of The Supreme Maulana from the holy country of Pakistan and we cannot fail him... we have to show these Hindus that we are not afraid of them – the Indian muslims are and that's why this show of tolerance – this will also give our muslim brothers in India a message that they are not alone – we are with them if they wish to fight..."

Chaitanya and Priya looked at each other not knowing what to do and kept listening, "we have a deal with a local leader in the administration – for 2 hours no police will be deputed that is by 10PM – we have to complete our mission in these 2 hours, inflict the heaviest damage and disperse – I hope you all have got half the money promised to you – the rest half will be given when the work is complete – you know where to come and collect it."

Suddenly Priya jumped keeping her hand in her mouth from screaming but the sound from her Payal and her Kardhani was audible enough to disturb the speech, "Stop – who goes there?"

Chaitanya grabbed her hand and started to run towards the back – he had seen a dump of soft sand for the construction on this side. He pushed Priya and then jumped from the sill of first floor on to the soft sand dump. He grabbed her hand again and ran toward an alley that was behind the building and at the first intersection took left making sure that they were not seen by anyone from that group.

"Why did you jump like that?"

"A mouse ran over my foot..."

"Women..." he swore beneath his breath and grabbed her hand and started to run again. He knew that the group would pre-pone the attack they had planned. They reached an edge of the alley they had now taken and opened to the entrance of the Mosque – they had just circumvented and reached the same spot again – only difference that the building where they saw this group's interaction was on the other side. He pulled up his camera and started recording the pelting of stones and bricks from that unfinished building. Suddenly two groups who rushed from either side of the Mosque to show that they had come out of it and raced towards the innocent crowd who reeled under the sudden attack...

"Come on – run – why do you want to record this riot – that too so close to the rioters?"

"This is a proof that it's not Indian Muslims who are rioting – they are Bangladeshi and Rohingya refugees led by some traitors and ISI..." he recorded the riot scene for another 2 minutes before closing the camera and grabbed her hand and started to run in the other direction and away from the riot... They ran with all their might and about 500 meters away were stopped by a group of muslims who were on their way to the riot location – armed with sticks and knives...

"Stop! Who goes there?" was the call and they were surrounded by 10-15 people.

"We are reporters from this channel..." he said looking at the readiness of those people, ready to drop camera and fight if need be...

"Oh! I recognise her – she is Priya Singhal – right?" he said suddenly recognizing her, "you must have seen what happened at the location – let us know..."

"It wasn't the muslims who prayed or who visited the mosque – they were somebody else who came from behind the mosque – seems like a planned attack to disrupt the harmony..."

"Hmm – we thought so – let us see you to safety..." he said and pushed them into an alley and they all started to walk – one alley to another, "Politics has gone from bad to worse – these people stop at nothing – any idea which political party is behind this?"

Chaitanya shook his head to convey that he didn't know, "How can we know? We were feeling proud looking at the harmony and solidarity between the two factions – suddenly this happened..."

"Hey" one of them said, "record that we are helping you to safety – that way a message will go to people that only a few muslims are like that – by and large we all are Indians... and it will also give us a chance to be on camera..." he said with a dream in his eyes.

Chaitanya put on his camera and started recording. Priya took the cue that this was working started to report how these muslim brothers were helping them out to safety – she wasn't sure about those people's intentions – she kept on reporting while he captured their faces...

"Any message you would like to give to the people of India?"

"Yes – we are Indians. We are not traitors. We don't know who has done this or who is behind all that rioting. I swear if we find him, we will end his political career..." one of them swore on the camera, "there you are – you are safe now... we are almost 1 km away from the scene. You can now safely go back – while we try and reach the place and try to bring some sanity to our brothers..."

They thanked them for their help and started to walk further down and away from the scene when the saw an autorikshaw – they asked if he would take them to the hotel. He looked at them and then ahead...

"You better make a run on foot in that direction – this place is also not so safe and pointed out to the people who were in process of burning down one of the shops –

they were about half a km away, "better go before they see you..."

Chaitanya grabbed her hand again as they made a run in the direction auto driver had pointed. They made their way through various alleys and away from the scene of riot. They were at an intersection of a main alley when they saw a crowd about 300m away in other alley and the crowd saw them...

"Hey – these may be the guys who we heard, they could know what our meeting was about – grab them – we will take them to our leaders..." one of them said and Chaitanya realizing the risk grabbed her hand again and started to run in the alley they had taken – the crowd followed them. She was good at running as she practiced to participate in various events of running and he had trained himself for army was good at running too – soon they made the distance between them and the rioting crowd and stopped at a junction where there were a lot of small warehouses. He looked at a warehouse that was open and led her to the warehouse...

He looked around and found that the warehouse was empty, the lock of the warehouse was still on the door with its key – the owner of that warehouse must have left in a hurry... "I am keeping the camera here with you and locking the door from outside. I am going to distract them into believing that you and I have now taken a separate alleys and I will return for you when it's safe – please don't make any sound or put on the lights while I am away and turn off your mobile – lest it rings – it's for your safety..."

Saying thus he closed the door to the warehouse and locked it from outside to make the crowd feel – if they reached the spot – that there was no hiding place there and they were on the run... He came out of that alley and saw the crowd looking for them – they saw him waving at someone to run in one direction which was opposite to the warehouses and looked at the crowd and started to run in the third direction. The crowd followed him in the direction he had taken.

It was almost around 9.30PM when the curfew was imposed by the government – the damage was done. The crowd had dispersed and everything was quiet. He looked around and found a bike with the key in the slot – someone had forgotten to take the key out. He shook the bike to check the level of fuel in it and found that there was enough of it to take them at least 100km away. He pushed the bike for some distance so that if the owner of the bike was around he wouldn't know that his bike was being stolen...

He rode the bike fast to where he had locked Priya she was sitting in dark and had pulled her legs up on to the table she was sitting. She could hear rats scurrying around and could hear them squeak intermittently. With every sound her heart beats increased. She was wondering what was going to happen to her if Chaitanya gets in trouble with the rioting crowd. She could bear it no longer – she also wanted to know that Chaitanya was safe. She put on her phone and called him...

"Where are you? Are you safe?" she anxiously asked him.

"Don't worry about me – any trouble? – I will be with you in next 10 minutes..."

He reached the warehouse to see about 4-5 people attempting to break the lock. He parked the bike and rushed toward them. They had been able to break the lock and enter the warehouse. They had put on the lights and when he reached they were near Priya...

"She looks hot and sexy – we can enjoy her here and then take her to our boss – what say guys?" one of them said and turned around as he heard a noise of the main door to the warehouse shut behind him. He saw Chaitanya at the door – he had bolted it from inside to prevent anyone else entering and was moving toward them...

"Oh! She has a lover too who likes to be heroic like film star - get him we will deal with our lust later..." and they moved toward Chaitanya who attacked them with vigour. After a couple of minutes of fisticuffs – they lay at the Chaitanya's feet – knocked out... Priya looked at Chaitanya in wonder as he started to click their faces with his phone. She was still sitting on the table with her legs pulled up. He signed her to get down from the table and gather the camera which had the information of ISI and their sleeper cell units which she deftly did, keeping a distance from the rioters...

Chaitanya hit them again with a force as they started coming back to their senses knocking them down again. He signalled Priya to open the door to the warehouse while he stealthily crept back looking for any signs of the rioters regaining the sense. They came out of the warehouse and he put on the bolt and locked it with an iron rod as the lock to it was broken. They swiftly moved toward the bike he had parked and jumped over to occupy the seats and vroomed off...

"Thanks for coming on time..." she said feeling a bit relieved, "where did you get this bike?" she wondered.

"I borrowed it... now keep quiet and let me drive you to safety..." and kept riding the bike. They found that arson was still on near their hotel – he turned the bike and started to ride again – this time toward the outskirts of Jodhpur. In the outskirts he looked around and found a shop selling helmets – he bought them...

"Where are we going?"

"To Delhi – our home..."

"What about our clothes and the bags at the hotel?"

"We can claim it later – as of now getting out of here is important. Those guys know who we are and will not be safe – it's better – we go to Delhi and seek protection from Mr Mahal... You ready for all night ride?"

"Let's have some food and then I will be ready – I am hungry with all that running we had to do..."

"First let's get out of Jodhpur ... we can eat at any dhaba we see on the highway – ok?" she nodded to his plan and they were soon on their way to Delhi. She knew she was safe and wondered that Chaitanya had so much strength and skill to fight off 4-5 people at the same time and knock them off – she started to admire him and his strength. It was almost 8AM when they hit outskirts of Delhi stopping only to refill fuel in the bike and driving as fast as the bike would take them...

CHAPTER FIFTEEN

FIFTEEN

They reached home and first thing was they called Mr Mahal to take his appointment... They told him clearly that they had no trust on Mr Das and wanted to meet him alone. So it was decided that they would meet him for dinner at the lounge maintained by army men and meant for the army personnel and their guests. It was Mr Mahal's birthday and he was treating his immediate officers at the lounge.

They were dead tired – first the running around and then all night ride from Jodhpur to Delhi. He said goodnight to Priya and crashed on his bed – she thought of changing but was tired too – she crashed on her bed looking at Chaitanya and thanking him in her mind for all the support and care he had for her – had it been any other person, he may not have been able to save her or take care of her the way Chaitanya did...

Though she was sleepy – she couldn't sleep – she was thinking of all the recent occurrences – the way she was abducted – the way Chaitanya had reached on time to save her – now this – their eavesdrop on the rioters – how her fright of a mouse had given their presence away – he had not been angry on her for that – instead had led her to safety. Then the point where rioters had got her cornered – he had fought with them and defeated them and brought her back to the safety of their home... she smiled at herself – little did she know that she was getting attracted to him. She got up from her bed and snuggled close to him and found comfort – she put her arms around him and slept soundly...

Hearing the doorbell ring – she got up and looked at the watch and then at Chaitanya who was sleeping a deep sleep. She blushed to herself and got out of the bed. It was almost 3PM and she peeped into the peephole of their flat – it was her maid. She let her in and freshened up while the maid did her work and left.

She prepared the tea and filled 2 cups of it and entered their bedroom, "Get up – you lazy bum – we have to meet Mr Mahal if you have forgotten..."

He lazily and tiredly looked at the watch, "Hey it's just about 3PM we are to meet him at eight – why so early?"

"We got to copy and edit the recordings we have and that's going to take some time. We have to camouflage the data we are going to give him so that it remains a secret that we gave him the data..." he got up and sat on his bed and looked pleadingly at her to go to sleep again, "here's your bed tea – sip it and start working..." she laughed at the face he made and moved into kitchen to cook some eggs for their breakfast.

He got out of the bed and freshened up and started working on the edits of the recording and made it presentable for Mr Mahal so as to save his time. Then he copied the data into a USB and put another USB and started to copy old songs into it and Priya looked at him in wonder..."You don't want Mr Das to get his hands on the data we have, right? – It will look like a gift to Mr Mahal on his birthday..."

They hailed a cab and left for the venue Mr Mahal had informed and reached there to see lots of families who would celebrate Mr Mahal's birthday... the birthday cake was already cut and was being distributed.

"What is media doing here?" Mr Das asked in astonishment.

"They are not media – I treat Priya like my daughter – can't a daughter visit to wish her father a happy birthday?" Mr Mahal came to rescue ... Priya as well as Chaitanya heaved a sigh of relief.

"Happy birthday Sir..." they said in unison and Mr Mahal accepted their wishes gracefully.

"Here's your birthday gift..." Chaitanya looked at Mr Mahal, "It's a collection of beautiful songs by Kishore Kumar. Priya told me you love his songs."

"Wow! Kishore Kumar? I love those songs too – with your permission, Mr Mahal, I would like to play these for all present here..." Mr Das interrupted Chaitanya.

"Of-course, you can play them for all of us over the sound system here..." Mr Mahal smiled, and Mr Das hurried to the guy who was in charge of the music there, "I hope that USB doesn't contain the vital data, Chaitanya?"

Chaitanya smiled and pulled out another USB from his pocket, "This USB contains the vital data – I knew Mr Das would fall for that..."

"Good thinking." Mr Mahal smiled and put the USB in his pocket, "You seem to be right – I will have to keep a tab on Mr Das... He could be informing the group doing all the mischief... How did you get doubts about him?"

"First time was when Priya got abducted... I had informed him so that I can get some help – but the abductors were killed leaving Priya unhurt – the most interesting thing is – we came back from that place and nobody found the bodies they were found distributed in an area of approximately 200 miles. The second instance was when we informed him about Radha Natekar and the money being put in her account through various unnamed sources – she was killed almost immediately as this news became hot on media... From there we were wary and started to contact you directly and we would like to keep it that way..."

"Hmm – so you have your doubts on him – he is with the group who could be killing all these people?"

"We have spread word around amongst the informers and promised 1 million cash from the amount you have offered to get this information – we are waiting for that info..." Priya explained.

"I am glad you could come out of that riot safe – where did you learn such fighting skills, Chaitanya?

"I have been training myself to join the army and have learnt not only physical endurance but also various fighting techniques... I tried for army but didn't fit in their physical standards. Since I topped every other field and exam as per their requirement, they have given 2 years to prepare for it and reappear for the physical test..."

"Oh! I see – but its good – at least it's serving me good. You both make a commendable team and I have full faith that you two will unearth this group and help us bring them to justice..." he suddenly started to laugh, "That's a good joke – really it is..."

Priya and Chaitanya took the cue and started to laugh as well – they saw Mr Das approaching their table, "That's a nice collection Chaitanya – Mr Mahal, even I love Kishoreda songs – can I copy it and then give the USB to you?"

"Of course you can..." he said smiling, "now join us for some drinks..."

After the dinner and the drinks they left for their flat.

"I will never drink with Mr Mahal, he is a tanker who can digest a lot of alcohol..." Chaitanya said with conviction – he was feeling a bit high and had to take support of Priya to reach the flat and crash in to the bed.

Priya was feeling happy that he had to take support from her and she felt good as she removed his shoes and took him to bed – he relied on her and he trusted her – she was feeling more romantic toward him... again she snuggled close to him when she went to sleep – he was already in dreamland...

CHAPTER SIXTEEN

SIXTEEN

She woke up in the morning in his arms around her and blushed to herself again and started to freshen up and woke him so that they can go to the studio for their normal work and duty.

They looked at the tasks given to them and started attacking them vigorously – she had to present the riots that happened in Jodhpur while he had the edited version of the footage and worked to present it for the news. She presented the version without letting people know the ISI hand involved and only suggested that there could be a foreign hand in these riots – even this prediction created a furore amongst masses...

Around noon when he was having his lunch and Priya was still at in the NEWS centre, Mr Mahal called Chaitanya, "Be careful – we have seen the evidences you gave and there is something to worry about – no it's not the ISI and the rioters – the people who cornered Priya at the warehouse – they are the concern – they belong to the same criminal gang who had abducted her few days ago – they have not given up – stay alert..."

That got Chaitanya thinking about the gang who was trying to harm Priya – who could they be? Which party is supporting them? How do they operate? Where all do they operate? How the hell did they know of her location? – It was a far corner of Rajasthan – not Delhi or UP – they had their presence there... he decided not to inform Priya of this, lest she might go into her trauma again...

It was almost 3PM when Priya was free from her NEWS centre and she was having her lunch. Her phone rang – it was one of her informer who spoke about Adil Khan – a leader who had been giving fiery speeches of provocation for Muslims to agitate – almost to a point to take up arms and law in their hand... he was to deliver a fiery speech or provoke some sentiment enough to disturb the social fabric of the nation. He was going to do this at a press conference held in Indore a couple of days later and needed to be stopped.

Priya approached her editor and asked permission to cover this press conference to which he agreed and asked them to fly to Indore and gather information. Priya told Chaitanya who asked their travel department – there was a flight late into night which was available and was booked for them as well the partner hotel at Indore which was the same venue where the press conference was to be held.

They left office early since they had to take flight to Indore and were awaiting the cab they had booked, outside the complex of the media house. Chaitanya suddenly noticed a sinister movement in the crowd and asked Priya to stand inside the gate of the complex and started to accompany her as if he had not noticed the movement. They had almost reached the main gate when 5-6 people started running toward them – they were almost close when Chaitanya pushed Priya into the gate and turned around to face them...

The first person couldn't comprehend what hit him of so sudden as Chaitanya punched him in his face – he was not expecting such a fierce punch. The second person had no chance as Chaitanya kicked him fiercely. The rest of them reorganized and made a formation around him. He was cautious to wherever the attack would come from – he suddenly made a move that they had not expected and made them come face to face again. He punched the left most person and moved toward the first person on his right – making them come to face him again.

One person drew a knife and charged at him – he deftly moved to avoid the knife but received a small cut and the blood started to trickle from the wound. He held the person by his neck and kicked the air out of him. By the time the balance two rushed at him and gripped his arms from both sides and prevented him from moving again. But he was ready for them, using his strength, he made them collide with each other and as soon as their grip had weakened due to the collision – he punched them hard. They were all on ground but recovering.

In the meantime, the channel had called in police for help and they reached the spot – 3 of them managed to escape but those who couldn't were captured and taken into custody. The channel formally launched a complaint for attacking their reporter and cameraman and saw to it that they remained in custody till the court heard their case and sentenced them to jail...

"You are hurt..." Priya said with concern, "first let's see a doctor before we pack up and leave for Indore..." she led him to the cab pressing her kerchief over his wound and they whizzed off.

They sat in the flight with a bandage on his hand – the wound was not deep and the doctor assured that he would be alright soon ...

They landed at Indore in wee hours and boarded the cab hotel had arranged and reached the hotel. She denied her room and preferred to stay with him in his room. She was now concerned – who were the people who had tried to attack her and attacked Chaitanya instead – just because he tried to save her? – He knew who had attacked her...

"Why did you deny your room? And where will you, or me sleep? – there's just one double bed in this room..." Chaitanya teased her.

"As if I don't sleep in with you in your bed when I am scared – I am scared right now and I find comfort in this room with you around me..." she innocently gave the answer to which he started to laugh.

"Chicken legs..." he teased her again – he was afraid as his feelings for her were changing from the time he had seen her in that Rajasthani outfit and wanted her to keep a distance from him...

"No matter what you call me – I am still going to stay put in this room and sleep in the same bed you are in – that will ensure my safety..." she said with a decision and he had to agree. Little did he know that she also was falling in love with him...

They had a day in hand and they decided to tour the city and enjoy the delicacies and fast food the city had to offer – the food street – was very much enjoyable. They returned to their room in the afternoon and bumped into a guy who was occupying the room next to them – the one that was left by Priya for Chaitanya's room... He was a bit queer, he just smiled at them and didn't say anything – normally people wanted to talk to Priya as she was a well-known face...

They ignored his behaviour and settled in their room for some rest... "Hey – we have been together since 6 months and are good friends – but we don't know much about each other – why not use this free time to understand about us better?" Priya wanted to know about him...

"Later – let's rest for some time." he said lying down on the bed and she joined him – soon they were in deep afternoon nap. They woke up in the evening and again explored the streets of Indore with her posing almost on every food stall for her Instagram uploads – she wore a red tight blouse that revealed her curves and a dark skirt showing her shapely legs. They returned with their stomachs full... They walked in the lawn of the hotel with her holding his hand to digest the heavy intake of street food they had... and then returned to their room.

"Now tell me about you – I want to hear it all..." Priya persisted on her noon topic.

"You are a lady and I have learnt that it's good manners to let the lady speak first..."

"Ok. I belong to Bihar..." she started and told him everything about herself – including her family, her school, her college, her first crush and her journey to become a reputed NEWS reporter, "Now your turn..." and wide eyed she waited for him to start.

"You have had a colourful life till now," he said looking away from her wide eyes with melancholy and began relating his past, "I don't know what parents are – or who my parents are... I am an orphan and grew up in an orphanage in Maharashtra. I don't know what religion I belong to – don't know which caste or creed ... I just know what the orphanage taught me – to be a human – to be an Indian – I belong to India and India belongs to me..."

"Sorry – I didn't know that..." she began but was cut short as he started to speak again.

"The orphanage was good, it had a school of its own and we studied in it – few lucky guys got foster parents – and few like me didn't. We grew up tightly knit together for we knew we only had each other to rely on. As we started to grow I decided that I would work for a government office – the advantage was – you get a pension even after you retire and that would help me share it with the orphanage. I wanted to be a part of the orphanage management after retirement and spend rest of my life for dis-owned children like me – even now I part with half of my salary which I donate to the orphanage."

"How noble and how kind..." she murmured trying to understand him better.

"While in high school, I started to research on the government jobs that were available – but to my disappointment – there were none. They were all reserved for the 'Special Category' – we didn't fall in them – the government has no reservation for us – the orphans. They have it for their vote banks... and again, the orphanage was run by a trust, the management of which consisted of so called 'Open Category' members – and that made it impossible to get a government job since they gave us an 'Open Category' name. Then I found that there is one government job for me – The Army. They will choose me for who I am and not for what background I come from... Since that day – I started to train to join the Indian Army – both physical and with education that is prerequisite to get into the officer cadre." he looked despondently at her, "When the time came, I appeared for the Army exam and topped it – I cleared all the basic tests but couldn't clear the physical test where the inflated chest had to match. I was short by quarter of an inch. They gave me time of 2 years to make it happen... To look after my needs I took this job as a cameraman in this channel where I met a wonderful girl and a human like you..."

"So when do you have to appear for the test again?"

"Next year – that's why you can see me working heavy at the gym – as well I also am practicing the martial arts – let's see if I can get through..."

"You will..." she assured him, "and if you don't – you can always be at my side using the camera." she smiled and looked at him, "I promise you that you will never feel alone and I will never ever let your background come between our relation..." they looked at each other for a couple of moments and she placed her lips on his and kissed him. This was sudden and he didn't know how to react – and he gave her one of the most amateurish kiss.

"What's this?" he was completely stumped by her kiss and didn't know what to say or how to react.

"Can't you read a girl's mind? – a girl will ask for your background only if she is romantically interested in you and wanting to marry you – and if you are who she wants to marry – you are a lucky guy – I have started to love you..." she said and pressed her lips again on his, after a small kiss, "unless, you are not interested in me or do not love me..."

The bulb in his mind lit up brightly and he looked at her and she lowered her eyes feeling shy to meet his – he held her and brought her close to him and kissed her, "I didn't know how to say this to you – but you made it easy – yes, I love you..." and he kissed her again – and they went in a passionate kissing session which turned into unstoppable lust and she lay on the bed with him on top of her... kissing with more passion and lust...

She woke up in the morning in his arms around her and blushed to herself. She freshened up and started to browse on her phone. He was still sleeping soundly and she occasionally threw a love filled glance at him. He had been a human and her protector – now he had proved that he was a MAN and she was happy about it. She gently woke him up.

It was less than 2 hours when the press conference would start.

He looked at her smiling face and smiled back, then looked at her aghast, "Do you realize, we had unprotected sex yesterday?"

"From morning I have been on internet and decided that I will have an I-pill so that I will be safe from pregnancy. After all this is over – we will talk to my parents and get married – what say?"

"Yes – only thing is they should not object..."

"Don't worry – they will adhere to the wish of their daughter – there will be no objection from them – I will convince them... Now get up and be ready – you got to set up your camera for the press conference."

He got out of the bed and freshened up – they ordered for breakfast which they had and then he kissed her in newly found love before making his way out with the camera. Their channel was not airing this live – it was going to be a routine press conference with channel's own inferences about what was said in the press conference.

She regaled in the glory of love she had experienced the night before and was sitting in a dreamlike state when she realized she was getting late for the press conference. She started to freshen up and went to take her bath. She was again lost in the dream of yesterday's love making as the bathtub water soothed her...

CHAPTER SEVENTEEN

SEVENTEEN

She heard a phone ring – it was from bathroom of other room she had left to be with Chaitanya and the queer looking shy fellow had rented it. She was amazed that she could hear the ring so clearly that it seemed from her own room. She wondered if the person had heard their conversation and the noise of love making they had – if this could be heard so clearly – he definitely would have heard all the sounds – and she blushed at the thought and ashen at the same time with the thought of the person hearing all the sounds.

"Chandrashekhar Azad reporting to Capt Laxmi Sehgal – we are at the venue since yesterday. Everything seems to go according to our plan. Waiting for the duck to emerge..." a voice – perhaps of the person who rented the next room reported to an unknown person.

"Good – take care that nobody sees you – when do you think the duck will emerge?" a female voice on the other end spoke with authority. He obviously had his hands were busy with something else for he had put the phone on speaker.

"Probably in next 10 minutes and we are ready for the duck. IED has been planted with the remote in our hands. Turn on the TV to hear his last words..."

"Good – check out of your hotel and proceed to Kharagpur – we have another duck, Shobhita Mukherjee and ask Ashfaqullah to proceed to Ayodhya – we have a duck who is a thorough criminal but has been elected to the assembly. Your instructions will follow..."

"Copy that – long live **Akhand Hind Fauj**..." the man on the other side of her bathroom said and cut the call.

She was trying to make some sense of what she had heard and suddenly realized that IED was an explosive and someone was going to be murdered with that explosive. She wanted to take a look at the guy next door but she was nude and in the bathroom. She quickly dabbed a towel to wipe off the bath water and wore some clothes in a hurry. She opened the door and ran to the next door but it had been vacated. The door was open and nobody inside. She guessed that maybe the IED was going to explode in the press conference – Chaitanya was in that hall – she ran downstairs without bothering to take the elevator. She was almost on the ground floor when she heard a huge bomb explode in the hall where the press conference was to be held.

She ran with all her might toward the hall only to see that it was filled with smoke. People hurt were groaning in pain of being hurt in the blast. Strangely, only the people who were on the stage were killed – all others near the stage suffered injuries – not the major ones but enough to land up at the hospital. She could identify her colleagues from other channels. She looked around for Chaitanya and found him hurt and wounded near the washroom. She tried to pull his arm to make him get up but he was heavy and hurt from the blast. She ran to the washroom and dabbed a towel hung there with water and started to clean his wounds. The wounds were not heavy but blood oozed out of them and didn't stop. The police arrived at the scene with a team of doctors and ambulances. They lifted some who were a bit heavily wounded, others were given a first-aid and asked to rest for a while – Chaitanya was among those who were given a first-aid...

"Good at least, you are safe..." Chaitanya said wincing at the pain he felt. She sat close to him holding his hand, "While you have time – why don't you go and get the I-pill for you?" he suggested and started to laugh but again winced in pain.

"I will definitely have it once you feel okay." she said softly somewhat trying to feel his pain which clearly showed in her expressive eyes.

"Don't worry about me – by tomorrow I will be okay and raring to go. Just need a night's rest. You take care of yourself – we have a lot to do..."

"You are right – we have a lot to do... will you be okay if I go to the medical shop for few minutes and return with your medicines and my I-pill?" she smiled at him and after a nod from him, left him at the reception with those who had received the first-aid and left for the medical shop. She bought the medicine prescribed for him and returned. He was able to get up and walk. She gave him a shoulder support and led him to their room. He lay on the bed and went to sleep as an effect of the medicine. She wanted to tell him what she had heard – but decided to wait till he felt better. She fed him the dinner and had it herself in the room after which he went to sleep again...

She kept looking at him blankly and wishing that he be alright by morning next day and sometime deep in the night, she fell asleep too. In the morning, she opened her eyes to see him sleeping peacefully. She freshened up and called for some tea, the room service brought in the tea and gave a parcel to her which was left at dawn by somebody with her name on it...

She was suspicious about who could have left a parcel for her. She grabbed it and ran her fingers around it to feel what was inside – she could make out that it was a thick file of about 100-150 pages. She wondered what could it contain – then was a bit sceptical about it carrying a bomb to kill her and Chaitanya. She kept it aside and gently woke him up – he was feeling much better now and freshened up – and had his tea.

She then related the incident of the day before when she heard this queer conversation of the man in the other room and how she had received a packet in the morning which was left by someone unknown and feared that it could be a bomb as well...

He carefully groped around the packet and found that it was something which seemed like a thick file of papers. She wanted the police to come and open it fearing it could be a bomb – but he said why would anyone want to kill them – it could have been one of her informers with some information about yesterday and he could have a clue about what was happening...

He prayed for a moment and started to open the package. It indeed had a file within – they opened the file and started to read the contents...

'Adil Khan – a fake leader and a traitor – this file contains all the misdeeds of him and with proofs. We are giving this file to you so that you can expose him and tell the people of India as to how dangerous he was to the nation. You are given 7 days to expose him or else the copy of this file will reach every channel...' the first page read. They looked at each other and started reading the balance file and what they found was astonished them...

The file contained everything – right from his childhood to the point of his rise as a local leader. ISI had made a leader out of him. His work was to provoke muslims in the country to rise in arms against all other factions of the society, propagate Love Jihad, promote the concept of Gazwa E Hind. This he did at the behest of ISI – all his work was dictated by ISI – in short he was an Indian born ISI agent. Then there were proofs of how he had taken money from ISI and funded the work. Where all had he spread the tentacles of his work. Who were his aides and accomplices – what did they do – how they used the funds to destabilize the nation, etc. The file also had extracts of his various impromptu speeches at various venues and with dates and times – how he was about to start a violent movement against the nation using the support of Bangladeshi and Rohingya fugitives – no matter who governed the nation... it mentioned who his ISI contacts were and what were their latest instructions...

They looked at each other at the information they had received. They decided to work on the report after their meals and his medicines...

CHAPTER EIGHTEEN

EIGHTEEN

"Let's go over the conversation you overheard in the bathroom the yesterday..." she recalled the conversation she had heard, "do you realize – this may be a secret government organization which is yet unknown to the people of India and they may be wanting to erase all anti-nationals – Mr Mahal could be aware of this and he has not said a word about it to us... he may be involved as well with this organization."

"I didn't think of this aspect – you seem to be right. He may be involved in this assassination. Else why would the informer single me out and give me the file of Adil Khan's misdeeds?"

"We got to find out what's going on – I mean the judiciary is left with no meaning at all – the law is only for a common man – the justice will be served by a bomb or a bullet to these traitors..."

"Let's keep this information to ourselves and see what happens to Shobhita Mukherjee or the so called MLA duck at Ayodhya..."

They rested for a day at the hotel to help him recover from his injuries and proceeded to Delhi. Before returning they asked the hotel staff if they could scan the cam recordings especially around the time of the blast. They saw the person who occupied the next room check out of the hotel – but he wore a low hat and his face was not visible. They inquired about him and were told that he was a tourist and was there for tourism. They even had helped him rent a car to visit the Mahakaleshwar temple nearby at Ujjain. He was registered as Chandrashekhar Azad in the hotel booking.

They made a recording of the report for Adil Khan as in the file and submitted to their channel along with copies of proofs that they made while at Indore. The channel editor also was astonished at this expose and the proofs and aired her bulletin on prime time cancelling all other issues. The nation was shocked at the expose as this was shown with the proofs. The people didn't know who could they trust in such a case and started blaming muslims of the country for producing such a traitor of a leader. The Prime Minister had to make a special speech to cool down the rising temperature in the country.

Ms. Shobhita Mukherjee was in Delhi to meet various leaders of opposition – she wanted to corner the government on some issue or their policy. She herself was under a scanner for a scam. Under the garb of an interview – Priya and Chaitanya met her and when they were offline – they cautioned her about the impending danger to her life – they clearly told her that they didn't know who the people were who wanted to kill her and asked her to be cautious wherever she goes. They thought cautioning her would help but she raised an issue that it was the current government who was plotting to kill her.

"Politicians," Chaitanya said in a huff, "you cannot trust them. They will try and capitalize on anything and everything which they deem would increase their vote share. Do you think we were correct in cautioning her?"

"It seemed logical – but the way she has reacted in every media will help those who want to kill her – simple – she is blaming the government and those people are free to do what they would do..."

"Should we inform Mr Mahal about this or what can we do?"

"Let's think – because if Mr Mahal knows about this secret organization, we would be in trouble – we have to be a bit ahead and know if Mr Mahal knows about this organization..."

They came to their flat and a phone call alerted them. Mr Rafique Shaikh, a sitting MLA in UP was arrested for murdering a family to extort them of the land they held. It was a case that was registered against him about 20 years ago and was reopened. Everyone knew he was basically a goon and did all kinds of crime – right from extortion to grabbing land to murders and illegal sale of arms and drugs... He was held by the law for the first time and he was being tried.

"Do you think this goon of an MLA is the duck those people were mentioning?"

"Could be – don't know yet..." Priya was short in her reply.

"What if he gets killed by that group?"

"I won't care – he deserves that – he has killed a lot of people in his lifetime – people who live by the gun die by the gun – will serve him right – I have reported many of his crimes and the then government failed to book him on any charges saying they don't have enough proof."

"If he is killed – we will have to speak to Mr Mahal and find out if this indeed is a secret organization belonging to the government..."

"Okay – let's wait and watch..."

A couple of days passed – nothing happened. They knew within them that something was being planned by the group. They decided to have a simple meeting with Mr Mahal and speak about anything and everything apart from the information they had with them... They met Mr Mahal at the same lounge for a breakfast, as they had previously for dinner and chitchatted about old songs and asked him of his old times. They even asked him if he knew any of the freedom fighters who had seen leaders like Gandhi and others and were quite impressed when he started relating what and how he had an interaction with freedom fighters in his early days. Even Mr Mahal had not seen leaders like M K Gandhi as he was born after they had reached the abode of the supreme – The God.

"Tell me Sir – I was reading articles related to Azad Hind Fauj...," Chaitanya started keeping one suspicious eye on Mr Mahal for any reaction, "Why wasn't any soldier from Azad Hind Fauj inducted into Indian National Army after the Independence?"

"Politics young man, politics in this country was always below the dignity. Those who tow the lines by it, try and achieve something but Azad Hind Fauj soldiers were not so lucky. Some of them were tried at Red Fort for conspiring against the British King and sent to jail. After freedom, they were released and called patriots but no compensation was awarded. They were sent home to fend for themselves. It's a pity about a force that fought so valiantly in Imphal and Kohima – the memory was erased within no time and without any noise..."

"I feel sad – for them... They gave us the tune for our National Anthem – they fought valiantly for us so that we can be born in a free country and they had to vanish without any trace..." Chaitanya said with his eyes still suspiciously trying to find one reaction from Mr Mahal.

"What is bygone is bygone – we can try and change whatever is in our hands and people like you and Priya are pioneers as you try to find the wrongs in the society and bring it to the notice of the people – people like us act on say of the government or if something dangerous to the nation is brought to our notice by our intelligence agents or people like you. We have to follow the law – there are many people who hold high positions and those who have a big clout – we know that they are wrong people – but we have to go legally and cannot take any step till we find enough proof to nail that person down. That reminds me – you people didn't inform me about Adil Khan and his misdeeds even when you were present at his press conference?"

"He was dead even before we landed up with the details of his misdeeds..." Priya said in a firm voice that surprised Chaitanya.

"Yes – we got the information a day after he was killed... We could do nothing but report it on the channel."

"Hmm – I wonder who could have killed him..." Mr Mahal wondered with suspicious glances still on him, "anyways now that he is dead – that closes his chapter... this could have been the deed of the same group who have been on killing spree all over the country – did you get any information on them?"

"Not yet – do you think Azad Hind Fauj could be active in some form as of now?" Chaitanya evaded his question and brought him back to the topic.

"Azad Hind Fauj – it was disbanded in 1945 when they lost the battle and surrendered – Indian Army had no space for them – and it vanished – the youths who had joined it were in age groups 18-30 and after 75 years they would either have died a natural death or if they are living – they would be about 90+ years of age – they cannot be active by any chance – what made you think that they could be active?"

In the meantime – Ayodhya was tense – Rafique Shaikh was being taken to the court. The police knew that this meant trouble – either by his own gang members or from a rival gang members – and utmost protection was given to him. They kept delaying the time he was to be taken to the court and kept changing the route of his travel to avoid any mishap...

The court was about 10 kms away from the jail he was kept – the roads leading to the court were blocked and the passage was kept clear. The police was keeping a watch on everyone who was nearby and were alert for any action.

In the vicinity about a hundred yards away truck and mini-truck laden with building sand were stopped at the check point and allowed to go to a residential building that was being built located in the 2nd lane away from the court but almost facing the court. It was built till 2nd floor and 2 more floors were yet to be built.

The security at the site noted the names of the drivers and the loaders in the trucks with their supervisor named Ashfaqullah.

"There's a request for only one truck full of sand – why bring a mini-truck along?" the security asked.

"The mini-truck is not for you – it's for a bungalow located not far from here and I am the only supervisor available today – so clubbed both the deliveries together..." Ashfaqullah explained to the security's satisfaction and he allowed their entry to the site.

Once the trucks were out of the security's sight behind the structure – the team got to work. They knew that it was a holiday for building workers and the place was going to be empty. He started to load a sniper gun even as he started to climb up the stairs. One person kept a vigil that nobody will go up the stairs without his knowledge. While other took spades and started to empty the sand from the truck. The security was suspicious as to why these people were using spades and the driver informed that the hydraulic system of the truck had failed which made them use the spades.

Ashfaqullah reached the top and saw that he had a clear vision to the court and its entrance. He was satisfied with the view and found a spot to rest his sniper to shoot. He knew he would have a minute or two after Rafique Shaikh is brought in by the police van till he disappears into the safety of the court. He adjusted the telescopic sight of the gun and patiently waited for his duck. He saw the convoy of police ringing sirens as they approached the court.

"Come on – he said - Rafique Shaikh, show me your face..." he urged and was ready to shoot him down. But, it wasn't easy, policemen were all around him and he had to be careful not to shoot any of the policemen. Rafique Shaikh gave him a chance – he stopped walking for a moment looking at someone in the crowd present there and that was his chance. With steady a hand he held the gun and pulled the trigger.

The shot was unerring – the bullet passed through Rafique Shaikh's head and killed him instantly. Ashafaqullah heard a small whistle signalling that someone was on his way up and looked below – he threw the gun onto the waiting mini-truck below where it was hidden by his men under the sand it carried...

He casually started to climb down – it was the security, "Nice structure – these flats should be about a 1000sqft – how much would they cost?" he asked the security.

"I don't know the cost – you can come in tomorrow and ask the sales team who sits here." and he moved on to check that everything was in order. Ashfaqullah climbed down the staircase and went up to the truck to see it was almost empty, knowing the suspicious security he urged his men, "Come on – empty that quickly – we have one more delivery of this mini-truck..."

The group then left the site and proceeded toward the so called bungalow again at the check point telling that they had made the first delivery and were heading for the other – and escaped without raising a doubt...

Chaitanya persisted on the topic, "No – I was wondering what happened to them because I was reading a book on them... perhaps as Intelligence Bureau thought you would have some information – wanted to meet at least one of them... "

"I believe we have some data on them – if you are keen on it I will let you know if anyone is alive and where you can find them... Just a moment – I got to attend this call... What? How is it possible? We have had no intelligence about this... This is not possible – get every man to track that sniper..." Mr Mahal looked astonished and frustrated at the same time, "I have news for you Priya – Rafique Shaikh is dead – he was sniped out when they were taking him to the court – obviously he also had lot of enemies – but this was a professional sniper who got this job done – a bullet right in his head - and this only means someone who is an army trained person – Indian or maybe a foreign hand – have to get to the bottom of this..."

Priya and Chaitanya looked at each other realizing that Mr Mahal had no idea and Rafique Shaikh was perhaps the duck she had heard the man speak about. He seemed to get busy with the event and wanted to work on it – they took leave of Mr Mahal and returned to their flat. They were surprised that a packet was waiting for them near the doormat. They opened it and found another file – a file consisting misdeeds of Rafique Shaikh... the same way they had received the file of Adil Khan after his death.

They went through the file and realized how dangerous was Rafique Shaikh's network and what all anti-national crimes he had committed. The file also contained photos, description and current locations of his sharp shooters, of those who handled his finance for him, those who led his drug and arm selling racket, his links with ISI – both internal and external. It was a vital data. They also realized that Mr Mahal didn't know of the group's existence and there would be another death – Shobhita Mukherjee...

They decided to tell everything they knew to Mr Mahal and make a copy of this file before handing out it to Mr Mahal. They called Mr Mahal again – he was busy in a meeting and said he would meet them again at the lounge in the evening. They recorded a report on Rafique Shaikh and his misdeeds and made a copy of the file, put the original one in the dickey of his bike and proceeded towards the lounge.

Mr Mahal looked tense as he entered the lounge and looked at them, shook his head and sat down, "I wish, at least, you would have unearthed who is behind all this – I am under tremendous pressure and the IB is under doubt of performance... Do something quickly – whatever amount of money you need to splash around is okay with me – but find the information..."

"We are sorry Mr Mahal..." Chaitanya stated in a low voice, 'We thought you knew of this group's existence – in fact we thought that this was a secret government group that's doing all these killings – but I think you should know of this – you may be able to save the life of a corrupt leader called Shobhita Mukherjee..." Mr Mahal looked at him in disbelief and nodded at him to carry on, "This is a group who calls themselves as *Akhand Hind Fauj*. They have taken identity of martyrs like Chandrashekhar Azad, Ashfaqullah (The patriot who was hanged for Kakori conspiracy in 1923), Captain Laxmi Sehgal the leader of Rani Jhansi Regiment of Azad Hind Fauj and are killing these corrupt leaders and anti-national elements who are threatening the social fabric of this nation... don't know for what reason are they doing this, but yes – they are doing it and cleaning India of filth..."

"This sounds like fiction... but go on..." Mr Mahal remarked.

"We don't know how many have been recruited in the group and they seem to know about everything – the file of Adil Khan revealed much of the muck he had been carrying on in his work. Now this file of Rafique Shaikh – it contains all the information – be it his goons, people who handle his money, people who fund him, includes his political friends, his ISI contacts – both within India and in Pakistan and elsewhere – that too with the proof... Their network seems to be highly skilled and as you said also trained in warfare and subversive activities – they know how to use a sniper gun..." he pushed the file in Mr Mahal's hands, "read that and you will know..."

"I will be damned..." Mr Mahal said after scanning the file for few pages, "Yes – it's got information with proofs and can be used to book these guys with various charges and send them away into jail for God knows how many years..." Mr Mahal was thinking about how professional this group would be and how deep it has it's operatives embedded into various systems of the country to find the information and gather proofs, "the file says that you have to report this on your channel in 7 days or they will find some other reporter who would do that – I will say don't disappoint them – report this – my way and we would be able to devise a plan to find them – they no doubt are providing a wonderful service to the nation – but the wrong way – they are not supposed to kill – instead they can work with IB and help us book people like these..." he then told them what to omit and what to represent in their news report and what proofs to be given to the channel to avoid any legal implications.

They left that copy with Mr Mahal and returned home feeling relieved that the information was in safe hands. She entered the kitchen and started brewing coffee for them and he followed her and sat near the dining table. Looking at her brewing the coffee made him dream of their married life and he slowly put his hands around her waist, "I hope you still have those pills..."

She turned around and kissed him softly, "Yes darling – I have those pills..."

"I can feel how wonderful is my married life going to be – with you by my side and brewing coffee like this..."

He turned off the gas burner and lifted her off her feet and walked towards their bedroom...

CHAPTER NINETEEN

NINETEEN

It was wee hours of morning – about 3:30 AM or so when Priya's phone buzzed. She gathered the bedcover on her naked body and walked into the main hall where she had kept her phone on charging and Chaitanya had suggested another round of sex after Indore... She looked at the number of the incoming call – it was a land line... Not knowing who the caller is – she answered the call.

"So you have good links at IB and you have told them about our existence..." a female voice spoke in a neutral accent. She was alert immediately knowing it was someone called Capt Laxmi Sehgal who was on the other side of this conversation.

"I know that voice – Capt Laxmi Sehgal is what you call yourself, right? – yes, I had no choice but to inform IB about your existence..."

"Bright Girl ! So I don't need to introduce myself..." the voice on the other side was cool and neutral, not giving away any accent to which part of the nation she belonged, "Good – I had anticipated this move and you played right as per our plans."

"What do you mean?"

"Isn't your cameraman cum your lover by your side?"

"No – he is sleeping peacefully in the other room – tell me what you want..."

"Now that IB knows of our existence makes our job easier and challenging at the same time. Now onward – you will get the information in advance – about anyone who is a traitor... Your job will be to expose him or her on your channel with the proof and get IB to arrest that person. If he or she is legally implicated, good enough – or else, if he or she manages to circumvent the legal procedure, we will kill the person mercilessly..."

"I don't understand what you are saying..."

"Look below the doormat of the main entrance to your flat and you will find a file – one belonging to corrupt practices and misdeeds of Shobhita Mukherjee and a USB of a filthy minister, Kantilal, who has his hands full of muck. Expose them and let IB take the legal action – if IB fails – its death to both of them..." and she cut the call.

It was about 3:45 AM and she knew nobody would be in the corridor. With the bedcover wound around her she opened the main door and sure enough – there was a bulge under her doormat. She retrieved it and closed the door. She kept the package of the files mentioned by Capt Laxmi Sehgal on the sofa and hurried back to Chaitanya who was still sleeping peacefully. She snuggled close to him and soon was deep asleep...

They woke up in the morning and freshened up – she was unusually quiet and he noticed it and asked her about it. She related the early morning call to him and he rushed out to the main hall and picked up the file and started to scan it...

"Let's hand over the file of Shobhita Mukherjee and Mr Kantilal to Mr Mahal – as Capt Laxmi Sehgal said – and wait for the action by IB – if not, wait for the action by *Akhand Hind Fauj* – we will know what is happening and who is true to our nation..."

"Ya – let's do that but let's go over the file of Shobhita Mukherjee and Kantilal – let's find out why they are on their radar... she is one of the top leadership in West Bengal and he is a cabinet minister in the current Central Government."

They started to go through the file on her and read how she used her tough goons for poll booth capturing and also had a hand in murders of many members of opposition parties – whoever looked strong in the region apart from her own party candidates were attacked and either killed or fatally wounded. There were proofs attached for every murder caused by her – the money spent on the goons. Then there were series of scams she was involved in and had embezzled loads of cash running into 9 figure count. She also was involved in coal smuggling scam and government recruitment scam where she had charged hefty amounts as fees to appoint the people to various posts. It also gave information about where she had hidden the cash – enough to put her behind bars for a long time... the file suggested that the investigation was not over yet and more misdeeds could be found – this information was enough to get her arrested and put behind the bars... Kantilal was a partner in the crime of scams and the proofs of where he had hidden the cash and other important documents was noted in the file.

Priya and Chaitanya made copies of the documents and proceeded to meet Mr Mahal. They discussed of what to represent on the news and left his office for the studio.

"Expose them on your channel first – the government will be under pressure from the public to investigate the matter and Kantilal being a minister in their cabinet – they would want to cover up the investigation..." Mr Mahal instructed them with what to report – the report would be enough to start the investigation without giving out every detail – the details of their misdeeds would come out after they were taken into custody.

They were surprised at the quickness with which the IB had acted – the case against Shobhita Mukherjee and Kantilal was registered – ED also was roped in for the corruption money embezzlement. By the time they reached home, the case was ready and the procedure had begun – both Shobhita Mukherjee and Kantilal were summoned by the ED and the same time ED raided their houses and their farmhouses to recover the cash. About 1200 crores of cash had been recovered in the raid along with 1500 kgs of gold bars and other expensive items. FIR was registered and both were taken into the custody.

They were held for a week when the high court sentenced Kantilal to 5 years of imprisonment, stripped him off the parliamentary member status and decided on bail for Shobhita Mukherjee till further investigation. Kantilal also reasoning that he was framed in this case applied for a bail and hearing in the Supreme Court. The ruling party sacked him from his ministerial post and their party. They feared people backlash in the forthcoming elections.

As soon as she was out of the custody, Shobhita Mukherjee started to work on erasing the proofs of other scams she was involved in, as well wanting to generate a massive public support in case she was arrested and sentenced to jail. She kept her goon force ready for protests and arson if the court decided to convict her. She was at loss as to how ED had the knowledge of where the cash and other items like gold were hidden.

She was going to visit Kharagpur for a massive rally in midst of the balance nation demanding that she be jailed for her corrupt practices and amassing illegal wealth. She knew if her hooligans and her supporters are out on street and have massive protests which will turn ugly – the court and the government will have to consider leaving her alone with no legal process initiated against her. So this rally was to gather the public support.

Priya remembered the conversation she had heard in the hotel at Indore – and guessed that Shobhita would be in danger of being killed by the group who called themselves as *Akhand Hind Fauj* – she had heard Capt Laxmi Sehgal asking Chandrashekar Azad to be at Kharagpur and the instructions would follow.

She along with Chaitanya planned to cover her rally at Kharagpur. They informed Mr Mahal and suggested that Shobhita Mukhrejee would be killed there. Mr Mahal informed them that he would put a force and ask them to be vigilant for any attack on her. They reached a day in advance and gathered information that the 2 rallies would be held during the day and in the evening – she would be addressing close party workers and would be having dinner with them...

Next day, they started to cover the 1st rally. It was crazy – thousands of people were attending it. She had a wide support from the public. Priya called Mr Mahal, appraised him of the situation. He assured her that his force was there and they were vigilant. They would nab anyone who posed a threat to Shobhita Mukherjee. They were dressed as common people. Chaitanya was careful to show the crowd keeping her speech from the podium in the background. Nothing happened during the 1st rally. They covered the 2nd rally and again nothing happened.

“They must have put off their plan as they said – if Indian government and legal bodies acted on the proofs presented to them – they will not kill her. If they fail to act – she will be killed." Priya inferred from the rallies.

"Not necessary – she is out on bail – not convicted – they may try to kill her. It would be good if they are awaiting the court's decision and not proceed with the killing. She has a massive public support and it would be a chaos if they kill her amidst any rally she is holding." Chaitanya observed.

They proceeded to the rally of the close party members to which they had an invitation along with reporters of other channels. It was to be held in a lawn. This lawn had an elongated building at one end meant for functions and the lawn was for the party of food and beverages. The structure was simple – the ground floor had a massive hall and two big rooms with a staircase that led to a room above. The room above was a simple room with attached washroom. This was for facilitating the bride and groom's rooms in case of weddings that took place there. The windows of these rooms were secured with bars and the glass doors to the windows were locked for the smooth a/c operation. The main hall was only on the ground floor – no staircase there, no structure above.

The lawn was completely covered by a shamiyana – a huge canopy made of canvas and white cloth supported by stilts of bamboo. It covered the entire lawn till the structure. The place was decorated with balloons all over with party's emblem and looked beautiful. Chaitanya looked at the arrangement and understood that it was impossible for any sniper to aim once the person entered the shamiyana.

He looked at Priya, "This place is secure – no sniper can aim at her once she is inside. The only place where a sniper can aim is when she gets in or out of this place from her vehicle. Else this place is safe, unless, they have planted someone in the close party members who will have access inside." He placed his camera on a tripod at the entrance to capture her arrival and shoot the footage of any sniper who might attempt to kill her.

The party members had already gathered to welcome her. The food for the dinner party was being prepared. She was supposed to address the party workers and then have dinner with them. There were about 500 important party workers who had gathered there. The balance workers were stopped outside by the security maintained by the local police.

She arrived with much fanfare with the party workers shouting slogans of 'Shobita Didi – go ahead – we are with you...'

She and the other leaders started to address the close party workers for what they had to do for the forthcoming elections. How they have to not only keep a watch on other party workers but also deter them from carrying out their plans to win over the public opinion. The party workers were pepped up and applauded the say of their leaders and Shobhita.

Once done with the address – they served liquor and started getting ready to serve meals. The line-up was Shobhita and few leaders had separate tables near the structure and the balance party workers had tables laid in a formation a bit away from Shobhita. The food had various dishes like fish, rice, sabji, roti and a sweet dish – Payesh. The food was delicious and people were busy gobbling it with liquor. Suddenly, Shobhita gasped for breath and fell down from her chair. She was lifted and taken to hospital – where she was declared dead. Dead from poison in the food she had...

Police immediately took all the catering people into their custody for questioning. They sent the food for testing to the labs. By late in the evening, the lab reports came in that food wasn't poisoned. Only the sweet dish Payesh served to Shobhita was poisoned.

"Now that she is dead – let's catch up on the action at the lawn where she was poisoned... we have had the same food, but we didn't get poisoned..." Chaitanya suggested and they left from the hospital where Shobhita was taken to the lawn where she had been poisoned. Priya started to ask questions to the policemen and the catering people who were held under suspicion. Chaitanya holding his camera started to scan the table where she had her poisoned dinner.

"Hi – I am Mr Mehra from CBI – I am in charge here." Someone announced and his team started to take the charge – the policemen were asked to stand outside the lawn premises. He approached Chaitanya, "I belong to the CBI and Mr Mahal has asked me to be in touch with you – you are Chaitanya, right?"

"Yes Sir." Chaitanya replied even as Priya joined him.

"Do you have any idea as to how she was poisoned – there seems to be no poison or any poisonous substance within this area – unless someone has carried it outside this premise – can I see the recording in your camera?"

They saw the people who were near her and the ones who had the chance of poisoning her. They made them wait and released others to wait outside the lawn premise with the police. They realised that all the people who were near her including the people who had served her the dinner were still in the premise. This clearly pointed that these weren't the people who had poisoned her – because if anyone had – he would have made a run, away from there...

Chaitanya's glance fell on the balloon that was immediately over where Shobhita sat – the thread seemed a bit wet as well it was different in colour.

"Excuse me" he said, "I will go to the washroom and be back." To a nod from Mr Mehra, he walked toward the structure and started to find a washroom. It was on the other side – so he climbed up the stairs to the room and entered the washroom there. He searched around the washroom for any trace of a poison but there was none. He looked at the window – the window was sealed with glass panes and a wire mesh outside it. He peeked from the window trying to guess where Shobhita sat when poisoned. He saw a similar dark colour on the white cloth where she could have sat and guessed that the poison was made to flow from the top onto the thread holding the balloon to one of her dishes. But he couldn't guess how – it was dangerous to step out on the cloth and canvas without knowing where the bamboo stilts were and if anyone had climbed onto it – had to be too light to be noticed. The bamboo stilt would have bent enough for anyone to notice that... There was nothing in the room – it was empty. The spot was about 10 feet away and walking 10 feet in a tight rope balance act with bottle of poison without knowing if there was a bamboo below the cloth was impossible. He returned to where Priya was and asking questions to people around – be it police, the security or the people held back for interrogation...

"I think – I know how she was poisoned – the only question is how it was administered..." he said looking at her blankly.

"What do you mean?"

"Let's talk with Mr Mehra and see if I have guessed the truth. That'll make me a good sleuth..." he said laughing.

They approached Mr Mehra and stood by watching him interrogate a person from catering.

"Mr Mehra – one minute please..." he said looking at the person walk away to the people who were being held, "I think you are asking and holding the wrong people... I think the poison was administered in a unique way."

"Do you think we are wrong? You have no idea of the standard procedures. Our job is to interrogate and zero in on who would have done it..."

"I don't doubt your procedures Mr Mehra – but look at the balloon directly over the place where Shobhita Muhkerjee was having her dinner. If you compare it with other balloons – you will notice that the thread that holds the balloon is brownish in colour and threads holding other balloons are white. There is a possibility that the poison flowed through the thread into the food of Shobhita Mukherjee."

"You have a good eye Chaitanya – you seem to have hit on the bulls eye – let's get that balloon down and send the thread to the lab for testing. Mr Mahal called in saying he was visiting the site and would be reaching the site in 3-4 hours. This was urgent and he wanted to know how someone had managed to kill Shobhita when such a security cover was provided to her.

Priya and Chaitanya left for their hotel thinking that Mr Mahal would be onsite in few hours and would take charge of the investigation. Chaitanya couldn't sleep – he wanted to know how it was done. Priya suggested they would meet Mr Mahal tomorrow – perhaps by then IB would have an idea as to how it was done.

Sure enough, Mr Mahal called up saying that his hunch was correct – the poison had indeed flowed from the thread of the balloon. Even he was thinking as to how could anyone administer that poison... He would be meeting them tomorrow morning.

It was about 3.30AM, Chaitanya couldn't sleep. He got up to a sleepy question from Priya. He told her that he was going to the site to see how it was carried out. She said that they could go there in the morning – he insisted on going at that odd hour because he thought whoever did this, may want to disturb the evidence.

"I'm not letting you go alone – I'll come with you." she said and wearily got out of the bed.

They went to the reception and asked if they could hire a vehicle to that lawn. The manager was a fan of Priya and offered his bike to them. Saying thanks, they hopped onto the bike and made their way to the lawn. The place was sealed by the police so he decided to circumvent it and reach the back of the structure and then try to get in... When he reached the back – he saw a huge tree outside and close to the compound wall. It had one of its branches almost touching the base of the square pyramid on the top. Chaitanya parked the bike next to it and thought for a while – it could have been the way – if the person had a rod or something similar about 20 feet long – the poison could have been dropped from the base of the square pyramid.

He decided to climb the tree to be sure, "You wait here – I will climb this tree and check out the location..." – and he started to climb the tree. The base of that square pyramid was quite high – the main base hall was 20 feet high and the room above had a height of 15 feet. It was dangerous climbing 35 feet with a risk of a fall. He carefully climbed the tree and reached the base of that square pyramid. The base had a narrow foothold about 9 inches wide. Perilously, he started to walk sideways on it – one step at a time till he reached the corner and dangerously turned toward the shamiyana. He smiled in triumph...

Priya was watching his circus with growing heartbeats. Falling down from such a height meant serious injury or even death.

"Don't move or look behind you..." a voice said and she knew that she was not alone.

"Who are you and what do you want?" she asked about to turn but then heard a click of a gun and stopped.

"Oh! So you have guessed how the poison was administered – Good! – Now we don't have to climb up again to get that bamboo down. You will do it for us – and to let you know we don't care if the world knows about it... We were outside your hotel when we saw you two on a bike and we followed you – we wanted to give you another file of Shobhita – containing some serious crimes she committed – and that's why we had to kill her – she deserved death. You will find the file kept on the bike you rode..." then there was a silence. Hearing nothing for a minute or two she tried asking few questions – but there was no reply. She turned around to see that she was alone again and the file kept on the bike.

Meanwhile, Chaitanya reached out to a bamboo shoot cut along its length, about 20 feet long. He perilously reached that and with his kerchief grabbed it and started to move back – Priya was watching him all the way, afraid that he will fall down. He climbed down the tree with great care and descended the tree. Triumphantly, he showed Priya the bamboo shoot he had retrieved from the top. They called Mr Mahal who instructed them to deliver to the lab and said he will meet up for lunch and gave the address of the lab to Chaitanya. They delivered it to the lab and returned to the hotel.

They couldn't sleep – they had another file of Shobhita with them... They started going through the file and what they found was difficult to believe. Shobhita ran a factory to convert Bangladeshi and Rohingya refugees into Indian citizens. They had identified at least 25 villages where she ran this racket. She had displaced the original Indian residents from these villages (about 10000 families) and nobody knew where they had vanished – she had placed her goons in their place. It was there that they carried out the dirty work. The refugees were given ration cards, aadhar cards with proper identities that proclaimed them to be Indians in various states. This enabled them to eat away a massive share of benefits meant for Indian citizens. They were taught different languages and sent to those respective states. The vote bank political leaders then settled them, building slums for them and feeding them with basic ration, taken away from Indian Citizens, which they needed for a living. The file gave them details as to who were those vote bank leaders involved in this racket as well it contained a list of aadhar cards with their names – the list was endless... To top it up, for the by-elections, she had nominated one of them (a non-Indian Bangladeshi) as a candidate of her party to the state assembly.

"My God! She really was a skunk of a politician..." Priya remarked, "Let's wait till lunch time and hand this information to Mr Mahal and wait to see what action is taken by him..." Chaitanya nodded his approval of this action plan.

CHAPTER TWENTY

TWENTY

It was noon and they met Mr Mahal who also was surprised by this information. He told them what to report in their bulletin and ordered an inquiry into the aadhar cards scam and the leaders who were playing the game of vote bank. He thanked Priya and congratulated Chaitanya on his sleuth work. He had been correct in solving the mysterious poisoning of Shobhita. They checked out of the hotel and returned to Delhi.

Priya got a call from another informer in her list – it was important. She cautioned the informer of what had happened the last time. He said that he'll drop a USB at one of the hotels. He also said that Bhavesh Kumar, a senior journalist and Rajkumar a probable candidate running in for the post of Prime Minister had hatched a horrible plan to usurp the current government. The 'Tool Kit' that they had received earlier was a basic one – this was the finalised version of that...

"Let's link each other's location on maps of our phone – that way if anyone of us is abducted – we at least will have the location of where they have taken us and it will be easy..." Chaitanya suggested. Priya agreed and linked her location with his and he did the vice-versa. The venue decided was Coast Café in Hauz Khas Village about 8PM.

"It's a romantic restaurant. Anyways – since the time we decided to marry – we have not had any romantic outing or dine out. I would love to visit the place with you..." she said and kissed him in her feelings of love and he responded with equal feelings for her.

Around 8PM they were seated at the one of the solitary corners of the restaurant, dressed up for the romantic date. The atmosphere there and looking at the couples – they felt more romantic. He looked at her in her eyes and his eyes showed that he loved her true. They ordered for their drinks and started to chat. The drinks came and they raised their glasses to a long and love filled life.

They finished their drinks and ordered for food when a couple sitting on the next table started an argument.

"I know what all boys want – I will not have a drink. You will get me drunk to have sex with me..." the girl flared up.

"No darling – it's not that."

"Well – I know boys – they are all the same..." she said getting up from her table.

"Look here darling – we do have sex even when we are not drunk – why the fuss?" he said getting up after her.

"Shut-up and get lost..." she said and pushed him away and he reeled backward towards the table where Priya and Chaitanya were sitting. He almost fell taking their table with him.

"Sorry for that..." he said to Priya and turned towards the girl, "Ok – we will not have any drinks – happy?" – The girl yielded and they went back to the seat where they had sat – everything was alright between them now.

Chaitanya looked at the table and saw a USB lying where the boy had hit the table. Looking at Priya, he grabbed that USB and quickly put in the pocket. Priya was nonplussed – the boy was not her informer. She looked at the boy calling someone on his phone and then turning toward the girl and holding her hand romantically. She received the call from her informer...

"Priya madam – the boy sitting on the next table is my son. He has dropped the USB on your table. Keep it with you..." that sorted the things out. They finished their dinner and returned to their flat.

He picked up his laptop and started to scan the USB – it contained Bahvesh Kumar's misdeeds. He realized that Bhavesh Kumar was a name in the 'Tool Kit' of what they had retrieved from the informer at Karnal. The starting slide of the USB said that earlier 'Tool Kit' was scrapped because many participants had been killed and now this was the final 'Tool Kit' prepared by a leader "Rajkumar" and the senior journalist Bhavesh Kumar. He started to inspect the contents in the USB with more caution. The USB first showed how anti-Indian he was... how he had twisted his words to create a riot in Behrampur. There was a muslim boy who was infatuated with a hindu girl and was constantly stalking her, messaging her and trying to talk to her. She was irritated and she complained to one of her friends, who was a member of a hindu political group who had helped her register a complaint with the police. They were going to bring the culprit and the police face to face because the police had not taken any action...

Then there was a recording of how he had asked goons to infiltrate the agitation and lynch the boy. When the boy was lynched by his goons to death – he had made an issue of that scene and proclaimed that the hindu group had lynched the muslim boy for his innocent infatuation. This had led to widespread riots in Behrampur and surrounding areas.

After a couple of months, there were riots at Bangalore run by a muslim fascist group and he had said that rioters have no religion – they are just rioters and had showed pictures creating more rifts between the followers of the two religions. He was a mastermind in creating rifts in the society.

"Isn't he the same senior journalist who was showing open gutters in a village when the entire nation was watching Chandrayan II mission and praying that it be successful..." he asked and Priya nodded.

Then there was a video which showed a hall and a secret meeting held there – it consisted of various people, all with their laptops. The so called senior journalist showed the Indian flag and systematically cut the Indian flag into 4 pieces in his slide to demonstrate his strategy and dramatically announced to the group ...

"This, my friends, is what you are going to do ... the key to win the election and put an end to the tyrannical regime of the current government – you got to cut the saffron from main stream and dilute the saffronization by castes and caste hatred, and he put on his next slide which showed many blocks of saffron – they each had different castes noted on it. He pointed to a group – this people are different castes and you got to make social media full of their struggle and create a rift between those. You will have to write and post intense and hate pictures and videos to get the communities to hate each other." Then he turned to other group – you got to make the mainstream as the scheduled community whose colour is blue and we will get support of the leftists and the Chinese. You got to show atrocities committed by the upper caste – you will have to write a script and make videos of these and circulate it in social media and youtube. We already have whatsapp groups ready for circulating these. He turned to another group - the middle class is defined by the white colour. These are the people who work hard to make their ends meet. You will have to create a content that suits them and show their strife – show how inflation is breaking their backbone and how the government has turned a blind eye to them. And finally, he said turning to the 4th group, instigate the green – the muslims that the current government is against you... how muslims are being categorically targeted by the government – unite them in hate against the current government. Then he went into details of how to do it and where should which group focus, how he will be guiding them... he also said that they were being paid advance of Rs.5,00,000 towards their services and will be paid another Rs.5,00,000 when the election is a week away and promised them a bonus of Rs.3,00,000 if the current government is defeated...

"This is crazy – everyone knows that the Indian flag consists of these colours but the definition of each colour brings pride that we belong to India. In the national flag of India the band of Saffron colour indicates the strength and courage of the country. The White band indicates peace and truth with 24 hour progress denoted by the Blue Samay Chakra in the middle. The band in Green colour shows the fertility, growth and auspiciousness and the travel toward the prosperity of this great land and a nation called INDIA... This person should be hanged in public for such scheming..." Chaitanya was livid with rage.

"This also tells us as to how much money is being spent... If they can spend about a million rupees only on social media – how much more on actors who will be acting in their videos and not to think about the goons and party workers who will also be playing a major role – if we can get this information – will be a good case for ED..." Priya chipped in...

They decided to meet Mr Mahal the next morning and apprise him of this – Chaitanya made a copy of the USB and kept it for Mr Mahal. He looked at Priya who now had a mischievous look in her eyes...

"You remember what the girl said to the boy in the restaurant?" she said winking at Chaitanya ... she started to run toward the bathroom as a safe place but he was quick and he grabbed her midway – she looked at him and kissed him signalling that she had yielded to his feelings...

In the morning, Bhavesh Kumar was heading toward one of his flats where he was working on a 'Tool Kit' of what the leaders of various opposition parties dependant on him were supposed to do – he had come out of that flat for breakfast and stopped at his regular paan shop for his favourite paan and also bought a packet of expensive cigars which he loved when he was thinking hard.

He then proceeded to the flat. He was supposed to finalize the 'Tool Kit' in a couple of days and was working hard toward it. The money he was supposed to earn through this was too much to resist the offer. He reached the gate of the building that housed his flat. A person bumped into him and asked if he was carrying any lighter or a matchbox to light up his cigarette – and he had one – the guy lit up his cigarette and drew a huge puff with a look of ultimate satisfaction on him.

Looking at that person his own craving to smoke gathered intensity and he lit up one of his expensive cigars. He puffed away at the cigar and felt satisfaction at the welcome smoke he inhaled. His flat was on the top floor – he took the elevator against the rule of the housing complex still carrying the lit up cigar. He reached his flat and was greeted by his maid who kept the flat clean and tidy. He passed on the keys to his flat to the maid who opened the door. She took a couple of steps into the flat and smelt a strong whiff of cooking gas. She ran to the kitchen to see what the reason was when he entered the flat. A huge **BOOOOOM** followed as the cylinder containing the cooking gas exploded instantly killing whoever was in the flat.

Priya and Chaitanya were still at their flat when this news was messaged to them by their colleague. Priya called up her editor who informed that the team was already at the site with a camera. It was sad that a senior journalist had died due to cylinder blast so was the maid who did the housekeeping for him. He asked her to come to office at her earliest and present the blast. Chaitanya had other ideas – he wanted the address of the maid's house and wanted to see their reaction – he had a hunch – if this group was behind this and she was not a part of the 'Tool Kit' – and if they were as patriotic as they showed – they will show up at her house... She told the editor that while the team was covering the incident she would like to capture the first emotions of the maid's house and show it on their channel FIRST – that will increase the TRP. The editor liked the idea and asked her to proceed. After few minutes, he called her up and gave the address of the maid's house. He kept the USB in her purse and picked up his camera and started their travel to the maid's house.

CHAPTER TWENTY-ONE

TWENTY ONE

Priya and Chaitanya reached the house of the maid. There they regretted the happening and started their interview. They promised that they will seek government compensation for their loss which cannot be filled up by the person but at least will give them some kind of respite as she was the sole bread earner in their family.

They were in midst of the interview when a government officer walked in... He said he regretted the death of that maid and was there to offer compensation from the government. He took the thumb impression of her mother and gave a bundle of notes – he said that there were 5 hundred thousand in the bundle. The poor mother of the maid didn't know whether to show her anguish of losing the daughter or relief of getting so much money in compensation.

Chaitanya thought – how come government agencies had become so efficient that the compensation was being given by the noon when the accident had occurred in the morning. His doubt on this so called government person was on the rise. He half believed that this was not an accident but the group had managed the accident and were unaware that his maid would drop in at the same time and were offering compensation...

"I'm going behind that guy – once you finish here – go straight to Mr Mahal – I'll meet you there..." saying thus he left her and started to follow the so called government person. He had seen it in the movies – he followed him keeping a distance that he couldn't guess that he was being followed. After a short distance, the guy climbed a bus and he had to rush to climb the bus. He was keeping a close watch – the guy was near the front door after buying a ticket to Connaught place while Chaitanya remained near the back door to keep his distance and play safe. They were passing near a railway line when he suddenly jumped out of the running bus – so did Chaitanya, and started to follow him again.

There was a train going to Gorakhpur which had slowed down and he jumped onto it – Chaitanya followed the suit – though in the bogie behind the one he had climbed. He started to move slowly through the crowd toward the bogie where the person he was following had climbed in... He reached the bogie which was connected and started to search the crowd for that person. He found him at the extreme end door of that bogie...

"You are correct – he has got brains – he has the attitude and he has the logic ... I will test him for his patriotism before I offer him the job..." he could hear the person talking to someone on the other end of his call. The person turned around...

"Why are you following me?" he directly asked Chaitanya this question.

"I have a feeling that you are from the group that calls themselves '*Akhand Hind Fauj*'..." Chaitanya replied looking eye to eye.

"You are correct in guessing that and for your health's sake – stop following me – you might land in some sort of danger – we are trained for this – you are not..."

"No way, until I have the answers to some questions."

"Listen young man – I am telling this for your own good... Leave me alone and let me go..."

"You have to answer my questions – why are you killing people than exposing them and letting the government agencies take care of them – why kill them?"

"There's no way out – especially, if they have a clout or are involved with dangerous criminals – they buy their way out or silence the witnesses – by following me you are putting your life in danger – shoo off..."

"I don't mind if my life is in danger – but I will not let my country be taken into custody by group who believes in killing people to clean it... there are agencies to do that work."

The guy looked at Chaitanya for a moment, "If you insist – the train is slowing down again – I am going to jump off – follow me if you want to..." and he jumped out of the running train – it wasn't that slow – Chaitanya took a deep breath and jumped behind the guy..."So you won't give up – eh? – okay, follow me and we will talk..."

Chaitanya's leg was a bit sore jumping off a running train like this ... but he followed the guy till they hit a small village. They sat at a chai ki dukan and settled down from all that chase and running around... "You realize we travelled a train without a proper ticket for almost a hundred kilometres..."

"Happens – when you are trying to save your country from enemies that are internal and the ones that are hidden – you got to take some risks. These are the enemies who do the dirty work and are more dangerous than the armies of enemy who attack you on the border – they can be seen and identified – but these bastards are hidden amongst us and help the enemies of the country... by the way you can call me Capt. Abid Hasan... not supposed to give away my real id and name..."

"Why have you taken on the names of martyrs who gave up their entire life to the nation? – you are but common killers..."

"Shut up..." the guy said curtly, "we are not insulting them – we are taking on their names to complete the dream they saw for Independent India... They had not anticipated treachery and we see it happen, everyday – to give them the due respect and follow their dreams – we take on their names. They are the most respected freedom fighters by us. Using their names, we feel proud and confident that we will be victorious – someday... secondly – you have been getting files from us. These files have a Tiger at the corner as our emblem. The Azad Hind Fauj had a Tiger leaping sideways – ours is a Tiger leaping at you – you never know how close we are till you are dead..."

"You are giving enough proof of what these people are doing to put them in jail for many years – why kill them?"

Capt Abid Hasan was about to answer his question when a bullet shattered the glass of tea on their table, "By GOD – traitors – they are behind you for the information you received yesterday and they were following you – now they have seen me... do me a favour – you see that sugarcane field? – run into that and keep running northward till you see a bus stop on the road – pray that they don't get you and surrender to IB – that's who you coordinate with, right?" he said falling on the floor and pulling Chaitanya with him...

"What about you?"

"Don't worry about me – I have taken an oath to die for the country if the situation so arrives... I will cover you till you get into that field..." Saying this he brought out a revolver and shot at the people who had shot at them… "Go – go – go…"

Chaitanya was a bit out of his wits – being shot at for the first time in his life. He quickly made his way to the field even as he heard more shots coming from two different directions. He ran across the field that covered him with its tall harvest and looked at the map for the northern direction… Soon he reached the bus stop mentioned by Capt Abid Hasan and hid at the edge of the field waiting for the bus. Soon he saw a bus arrive and saw it was headed to Delhi – he quickly emerged out of the field and boarded the bus and heaved a sigh of relief.

About 5kms away from that bus stop, he got a seat and was about to call Priya to tell her of his adventures when the bus suddenly screeched to a halt. Few men dressed in uniform boarded the bus and started to scan every person sitting there. He thought that they were there to check for Capt Abid Hassan – he was wrong. One of the men in uniform approached him and pointed his gun at him, "Come with us quietly – we don't want any trouble to the passengers…" and Chaitanya quietly got up from his seat and got off the bus.

They pushed him into an army jeep and started to cruise, "Where is your accomplice who shot at us?"

"Who? – I am alone and I work for a NEWS Channel. I have nobody accompanying me…"

"Oh! Yeah! – we will know very soon of what you have been scheming… be at rest while you can…"

They halted at a desolate house not at an army camp or a police station – which made him suspicious. They prodded him to enter without speaking and he entered the desolate house. He was made to sit on a chair – he didn't know the chair was actually made for torture. They clamped his hands and waist to the chair while a huge screw behind his back was the main torture weapon – it was used to screw anyone sitting in that chair to break the backbone and render him immovable for life...

He sat there waiting for the torture to begin. He knew he was caught up in something deep and didn't know who to trust. These men seemed from army or one of the special security forces of IB, NIA or RAW... After an hour or so, Mr Das appeared at the scene and smirked at him.

Priya was concerned – she had finished the interview long back and was waiting for Chaitanya to return. It was almost 2 hours – she decided to meet Mr Mahal in case Chaitanya was in danger and also as per the plan given by Chaitanya the USB had to be given to Mr Mahal. She hailed a cab to Mr Mahal's office – he was not in his office – he was in an important meeting with the NSA Chief. After a half hour's wait he entered and seemed livid with rage. Priya sat in his cabin as he summoned Maj Nair...

"Where is Mr Das?"

"Sir – don't know – he has gone out without security even when I insisted – he said don't bother about my security – I will take few guards with me..."

"Find his bloody location – I want him traced with next 15 minutes..."

He turned to Priya – "What is the NEWS? – give me a good one – I am sick of bad ones..."

"Here is a 'Tool Kit' – made by Bhavesh Kumar who now is dead and a leader who probably will run for the post of Prime Minister in coming elections 'Rajkumar' ..." she handed the USB to him and then looked a bit concerned, "Is everything alright?"

"NO – the ED chief just informed me that Mr Das has a brother-in-law who has received a sum of 50 million from an unknown source – I want to find out WHY..."

"Another NEWS of concern – We think, we met a person from the group called *'Akhand Hind Fauj'* and Chaitanya went off to follow him – he has not yet returned – it's been almost 3 hours now..."

Maj Nair knocked on the door for seeking entry and was beckoned in by Mr Mahal, "Sir we got the location of Mr Das via his phone – he is about 100 kilometres away from Delhi..."

"What is he doing there?"

Priya suddenly realized that Chaitanya and she had shared each other's location on the map. She quickly looked at her phone map and saw his location... He was somewhere near Bulandshehar a bit away from the road leading from Delhi... She told his location to Mr Mahal...

"Mr Das is on the same way and has almost reached Bulandshehar..." Maj Nair informed, "He maybe there to meet up Chaitanya..."

"No way – he doesn't trust him a bit." Priya said this with conviction, "he will never contact Mr Das for anything..."

"I think Chaitanya is in danger and Mr Das could be at the bottom of his disappearance ... Maj, Call a squad from special security force and we together will go to the spot – Priya give me your phone so that I can track Chaitanya..." Mr Mahal finally decided.

"I am coming with you."

"No dear – it could be dangerous – I can't put you in danger..."

"Still – I am coming with you..."

After a pause and looking at her determined glance Mr Mahal yielded and consented that she comes along with them. The squad from other end of Delhi would take approximately the same time they would take from their office. Soon, they were on their way to Bulandshehar.

Mr Das looked at Chaitanya and slapped him, "So you are the informer of the group that's killing people..."

"No – I am the one who's trying to find the truth and the people behind all these killings..."

"Did you receive a USB of a 'Tool Kit' planned by Bhavesh Kumar and Rajkumar – do you have it with you?"

"No - haven't received anything ..."

Another tight slap followed from Mr Das, "Do not try to hide. We caught the informer and he told that he has given it to an unknown person who gave him a 100 thousand for the information. Another copy he said he had asked his son to give it to Ms Priya – we don't know if she has got it – and I am sure she'll give to me like last time... It wasn't difficult to make him speak – two tight slaps and he was speaking like a parrot... So who is this unknown person who received the USB if not you?"

"I don't know." Chaitanya replied and was kicked in stomach as a reply...

CHAPTER TWENTY-TWO

TWENTY TWO

Priya was now really concerned as to what had happened to Chaitanya – she kept praying that he be safe. She looked at grim faces of Mr Mahal and Maj Nair and her concern grew...

Mr Das was torturing Chaitanya for the USB that was with Priya. He was twice searched physically for the USB but it wasn't with him. After receiving another box on his face from one of the men in uniform – he finally asked Mr Das...

"What is in that USB that you are so inclined to torture me?"

"It contains final 'Tool Kit' on how to divide the country so that Rajkumar wins the elections. Yes it would take the country few years backward but it's nothing to worry about – it can be contained and to speak about the riots that will happen – nobody cares if a few thousands of people die – it's good for the overpopulated country..."

"You are sick – what's in it for you?"

"Rajkumar has promised me that all the chiefs of the government agencies like IB, ED, NIA will be replaced by his nominated persons and I as NSA chief will be heading them... A good reason to be loyal to him... These are not soldiers or police – these are goons of Rajkumar – now you understand where we stand and how much of trouble you've gotten into..."

"What do you think – your plan is going to work? – keep dreaming..."

"Aren't you afraid of death?"

"If I have to consider my life to the health of this nation – my life is nothing – there are I believe many more people who won't consider their lives to be precious than this great nation called India..."

"Ok – your choice – suffer more torture – I promise – tell me who those people are and where the USB is – it will be a simple and painless death – why do you want to endure so much of torture?"

One of Mr Das's goons punched him more around his stomach area – they also hit his legs with batons – but he was silent and started laughing, "I can see your frustration – I want to see you get more frustrated before you kill me. I wanted to join the army which I couldn't but I feel as if I am caught by the enemy who is torturing me for information – I am playing my part of my dream."

Mr Das could take it no longer – he pulled out his revolver and brought it close to his forehead where he could see through the nozzle, "Out with the information or you die..."

"Are you done with your patience? – I am glad that I won – I could endure enough torture than you could hold your patience to get frustrated enough to kill me..." he laughed out again, "How will you run the government agencies if you are so low on your patience?"

"You..." Mr Das almost choked and hit his forehead with the butt of his gun and Chaitanya passed out, "Splash him with some water and bring him back to his senses – I want to know who else does possess that USB..." he said to one of his goons.

They got a jug of water and splashed on his face. He slowly came back to his senses and looked around and saw Mr Das's face and smiled at him, "You still at my torture? Must acknowledge your persistence ..." he said weakly.

"Are you going to speak up or do you want me to increase the torture to the next level where we starting cutting off your fingers – one by one. Last time you were able to save Priya when we abducted her by killing our people – who is going to save you? – you definitely are not banking on Priya for the same action – she's just another sexy doll and won't be able to save you..."

"Oh! So it was you and your goons who had abducted her and I kept wondering who would have done that cowardly thing..." he was now playing with Mr Das's psyche by chiding him. He had taken so much beating that he no longer cared if he was killed by these goons – he was enjoying frustrating Mr Das...

"You don't realise – this is an old fashioned torture chair – it can be very uncomfortable and can maim you for life – we will not kill you but torture you enough to break your backbone and render you useless to enjoy your life with that sexy babe of yours..." saying this Mr Das turned the torture screw till it touched Chaitanya's back. Chaitanya winced, as rather than the screw, the pain of being hit on stomach and his legs now was on the rise, "You cannot bear the screw even this much? – wait till it starts hurting you..." and he turned the screw more to poke his back till it pained.

"Kill me if you can – but I will still say that the USB is not with me..." Chaitanya said realising that one more copy which Mr Das was mentioning must be with *Akhand Hind Fauj* because Bhavesh Kumar was killed – he realised that it was a planned accident. Unfortunately name of Mr Das didn't feature in that USB – it was just noted that a senior officer from IB was involved... he knew that sometime later on the justice will be delivered and Mr Das will be killed – though he may not be alive at the time of justice...

The door to that room opened and Mr Das looked irritant, "What's the matter – can't you see I am busy..." and he turned the screw further to hurt Chaitanya.

Few bullets were fired and Chaitanya saw the goons falling dead around him and wondered who it could be who was now shooting at Mr Das's goons – was it some other opposition party who wanted to hijack the 'Tool Kit'?

"Mr Das – no sudden moves – raise your hands and move to that corner slowly..." a voice of a lady could be heard.

He looked patiently as Mr Das took the position he was asked to without a word – his hands raised, scared and nonplussed...

"That's good," the voice carried on as she unscrewed the screw that was hurting Chaitanya, "We were wondering who that senior person from IB was, who was a traitor – now we know it's you..."

"Who are you now? – it's like frying pan into the fire – now maybe it's your turn to torture me..." Chaitanya said with dejection that his torture will start all over again...

"Don't worry – we are not here to torture you – I am Capt Laxmi Sehgal. After you started to run away from Capt Abid Hasan, he was surprised to find the attackers follow you instead of him – so he followed you and found you captured by these men and instantly alerted us and we knew they would be trying to get information about us from you which you don't know... We heard these people torture you – you are brave, I salute your courage – you didn't mind your life was in danger but faced the torture. You could easily have told that the USB was with Priya with instruction to pass it on to Mr Mahal. You could have given us away ... You are a true patriot."

"How do you know that?"

"Capt Abid Hasan was not the only person present there at the maid's house – we had planted another person who kept a watch on everything – we knew you were following him and asked him to speak to you – but you both were attacked before he could speak to you..."

"So – what took you so much time to reach here?"

"One we had to eliminate the guard around this place – it wasn't easy because this place is in the open and they could see us approach. Secondly, we wanted to be sure that you were not in league with Mr Das and not a traitor."

"Oh! I see... now will you free me off this chair – I want to rub on the wounds these people have given."

"Not now – we don't know if you are on our side as well – so you will have to wait till someone comes and releases you..." she turned to Mr Das, "Das – you had a good position in IB and would have become IB chief in 4-5 years when Mr Mahal would have retired – what made you so greedy?"

"He was going to be offered a Chief of NSA position by Rajkumar if he won the election and became the Prime Minister of Inida..." Chaitanya gave information to see the reaction.

"Oh! Did you believe that Rajkumar would keep his promise? He is multi-standard liar – he will already have planned what he wants to do – his politics is dirty so is he..." Chaitanya was listening to her speak to Mr Das and saw an expression of extreme fear on him, "Now that you have done treachery with the nation – you don't deserve to live Mr Das – Good Bye..." and a bullet was shot and hit him straight in his head killing him instantly.

"You people seem to be patriotic – why do you kill people which turns you into criminals?" Chaitanya wondered.

"Yes – we are patriotic. We kill people to keep this nation safe from traitors. These are the people who have no right to be alive in India."

"Why don't you let the government agencies handle these affairs – you seem to have proofs of their misdeeds..."

"We have tried that – and you have the proof – we did let you know about Shobhita Mukherjee – what happened – she got a bail from the court – and she had all the time in the world to play around and disturb the proofs we had collected. The factories set up by her had to close down as there was no legacy who could run those factories where Bangladeshi and Rohingya muslims were given Indian identity to make them Indian citizens. Now who else is doing that – we will find out and kill them too... The government agencies have a protocol – they arrest the person and produce him in the court – then its court's decision whether to convict or to let him out on bail – most people who are politically influential get bail and then they play around with the proof and get released as the agencies don't have enough proof to nab and convict them... That's where we come into the picture – they can convince the court but not us – we know of their misdeeds – and we provide justice to people of India – eliminate them from the face of this earth..." she said giving it a simplicity of nature to their killings.

"But – still – you could give the government some time and help them with the proofs – you seem to be organized and have inroads where government agencies don't – that's why you get these proofs – people don't know who you are, how you look or who your next target will be... give them a chance..."

"If you see – we have started giving a chance to government agencies a chance by giving you the proofs which you hand over to Mr Mahal of IB special internal security – he is an honest officer and tries his best – but can you predict if the court will grant a bail to the person? – well we cannot take chances – it's our nation that is at stake..."

"So you will keep killing these high profile people."

"Yes – for our nation – we will keep doing it till the legal structure is made for fast trials and justice – not giving bails at 3AM..." her voice turned softer, "you are as patriotic as we are – we saw that even today when they were torturing you – you have a strong body that needs training and you do have brains and that's what we like – you proved it when you discovered how Shobhita was killed ... I want you to join *Akhand Hind Fauj* ... think about it ... with all these skills and information network of your girlfriend Priya – you can soon be at a good rank. We can compensate you with a good package and you will work toward making India a safe country..."

"Where do you get you funds?"

"We have many rich people and industrialists who are as patriotic as you and who don't want to be known – rather than give black money to these dirty politicians – they provide us with funds – you will be surprised if we name them... further we have NRIs both rich and well to do, who donate to our cause... Further, we also loot these corrupt politicians of their black money..."

"How do you hide all that money from the government?"

"You want all answers now? – That too before joining us? – you got to do better than that Chaitanya... now here's the deal – you take your time and decide to join us or carry on as you are – both ways it's going to be beneficial to the nation – we need honest reporting in the media which has now become filthy. And one more thing – you think we are afraid to let you know of our target and that IB will be able to save them – hear this – we are going to kill Rajkumar tomorrow when he attends his political rally – and even if he doesn't – he still will be killed tomorrow – he is dangerous to the nation – not only he is one of the masterminds of the 'Tool Kit' – he also is affiliated with China and other foreign agencies who are against India... I am keeping a file of his misdeeds on this table behind you for you to decide if we are right in killing him – do not forget to see him get killed – once we are out of here we will contact IB and tell them about your location and they will rescue you and recover these bodies..." – a soft whistle was heard and a person entered the room...

"Captain – it seems IB has his location – they are almost here. It's not safe to hang out here anymore..." the person informed.

"Okay – we got to go now – think about my proposal – we will be in touch with you – anyways... take care..." she said this and there was silence – the group had left without noise as they had arrived... Chaitanya had a long wait – almost 30 minutes which seemed like eternity before the IB team arrived...

CHAPTER TWENTY-THREE

TWENTY THREE

Priya was now really concerned as they approached his location – he hadn't moved from that location for quite a while now – she feared that something bad had happened to Chaitanya – perhaps – even more, worse...

Even as they approached his location – Maj Nair pointed out that Mr Das was at the same location. They were met by the squad from special security forces of IB and they discussed a plan of approaching the structure. Mr Mahal and Priya were asked to wait in the car till they found the location to be safe for them... In a formation, they started to approach the structure. They were surprised at the dead bodies around which were fresh – feeling more confident, they moved in for the action – but there was none. They found more dead bodies inside the structure including that of Mr Das.

They called Mr Mahal in and Priya accompanied him – they looked at the ghastly picture of dead bodies of which Priya confirmed two who had attacked her in Rajasthan. They rushed in to find dead body of Mr Das and alongside in the torture chair, Chaitanya was senseless. Mr Mahal touched his neck and confirmed that Chaitanya was alive – they removed the clamps that fixed him to the chair and gently woke him up. Priya was in tears when she saw his plight. He had received major bashing during his torture;

the screw that hurt his back was still protruding from the back of the chair...

"What happened here?" Mr Mahal asked looking around.

"Mr Das is the traitor and the mole you are looking for – it's him who tortured me for the copy of USB that contains 'Tool Kit' by Bhavesh Kumar and Rajkumar." Chaitanya could hardly speak due the pain he endured but carried on, "I was saved by *Akhand Hind Fauj* soldiers. It's they who killed Mr Das and his goons."

"You can't call killers soldiers Chaitanya..." Mr Mahal vehemently disliked the idea, "These kill Citizens of India – soldiers guard people and the sovereignity of the nation..."

"These are soldiers who are killing traitors – but without recognition by anyone..." Chaitanya passed out again.

Mr Mahal shook his head, "This guy seems to have endured immense torture by Mr Das – let's take him to the military hospital – we will talk when he feels better..." They took him to military hospital and Delhi where he was treated for his wounds. In short time, he was feeling better and wanted to go home – the doctors after a short argument allowed him to go... Mr Mahal asked them to join them to dinner and they joined him...

"What happened there?" Mr Mahal asked chewing on a piece of chicken.

"We went to the maid's house thinking that nobody would think of interviewing her family. A man came and said he was from the Government and offered compensation in cash... That got me thinking – how come Government has become so efficient that within 2 hours their representative comes and delivers compensation – that too in cash whereas we have covered stories about families who had to make several rounds to the government offices to get the compensation. The minister or a local leader then takes the credit for that and then we find out that either the cheque is not signed or bounces..."

"You are correct – government machinery is not so efficient that within 2 hours the compensation would be provided."

"This got me thinking that the guy must be from the *Akhand Hind Fauj* and I started to follow him – we took a bus then climbed into Gorakhpur express which had halted at a signal – then we jumped from the running train which had slowed down at a signal – I had caught up with him – he introduced himself as Capt Abid Hasan – a name of a brave soldier from Azad Hind Fauj. From him I came to know that Bhavesh Kumar was killed by them via gas leak which was made to happen but before we could converse, people with guns attacked us – he asked me to run and take cover in a sugarcane field and gave me the directions to reach a bus stop where I could board a bus going to Delhi – while he shot back at the guys and provided me with fire cover..."

"Hmm – interesting..."

"I boarded a bus going to Delhi but was caught by men in uniform who later I understood were Mr Das's goons ... Mr Das worked for Rajkumar and was inquiring about what I had done with USB that contains the 'Tool Kit' – we had not told him about the USB and neither you knew of its existence – I had asked Priya to hand it over to you once the interview was done and I was to join her at your office. Mr Das was promised the position of Head of NSA by Rajkumar if he joins him and he was misusing the powers he had with IB – he was the one who sent goons who abducted Priya in the first place. It was *Akhand Hind Fauj* persons who rescued her as well they rescued me..."

"What do these people want?"

"I had a discussion with Capt Laxmi Sehgal – she said that anyone who misuses the power or works against the nation would be killed by them – it's their job – many people have been recruited – they have NRIs as well rich nationalistic people in India funding them – they also loot the illegal money from the corrupt – Shobhita Mukherjee was an exception because they wanted her arrested – else all her black money would have been looted – it wasn't a small amount you know that... and these corrupt people will not complain of this theft for they will have to face an inquiry as to how they got such money in first place. They killed Mr Das and his goons and said they will inform IB of the location where I was being held – but one of them informed that IB was on its way to the location and they left. They said "Don't forget to watch Rajkumar killed tomorrow during his rally..."

"Oh! My God – another killing and that too of a prominent leader... I got to ensure that he doesn't reach the rally."

"No use – they said that this is a challenge to all security agencies – they would still kill him tomorrow even if he doesn't attend the rally – he's too dangerous for the nation..."

"What do you think of them?"

"They are doing what government agencies are supposed to do – identifying all those who are dangerous to the nation... They are patriots and doing a fine job..."

"If you were an IB soldier – I would have court martialled you for this statement. Killing people is criminal – bringing them to justice is right – they should do that and earn handsome money from IB and other agencies... just like your informers do..."

"That exactly is the point said by Capt Laxmi Sehgal – she said that henceforth after they kill Rajkumar – they will try to bring such people to justice – but if the justice fails – they will deliver justice by killing that person."

"We will provide the justice – don't worry about it. Did you see her face?"

"Nopes – she stood behind me all the time we discussed. But I will not forget her voice. Anytime she is around and is speaking – I will be able to recognize her – I saw her shadow and roughly know her stature..."

"I want you to be at the command centre tomorrow – at the time of the rally. We will keep our agents – both male and female and there will be many CCTV cameras as well drones that will cover the event if Rajkumar still carries on with his plan. You try and identify her... we can stop them from committing more crimes and negotiate for how we can save them from punishment – if they cooperate with IB."

"Okay – I will be before the road show – what time is the rally?"

"5 PM..."

They all had forgotten about the file on Rajkumar – Chaitanya hadn't... He took the file along with him to home while Priya was careful to nurse his sore points. Once they had their dinner, Chaitanya sat with Rajkumar's file...

"Don't you want to sleep and rest?"

"No – come here – I am going through Rajkumar's file." he said and she sat near him as they carefully went through the file. It contained the proofs of corruption by Rajkumar and the money embezzled was too much for any person living on this planet. The file also revealed his secret account in Swiss Bank and Bank of Hong Kong – it was supposed to contain more money than the proof of corruption. He had secret links with ISI and ISIS which he used to spread terror attacks around the country as a tool to further his political ambitions. He had taken huge amounts from China and few other countries with an assurance that when he comes to power – he would favour them with trade and infrastructure projects thus giving them an opportunity to collect the money back. He also had given China few military secret documents in return of the favours... further he was a mastermind of a brilliant 'Tool Kit' to divide India and create such rifts amongst Indians that the whole country could burn in arson. It was a deadly plan...

"No doubt – *Akhand Hind Fauj* wants to kill him. Let's see – if we give these proofs to Mr Mahal – would he be able to put him behind bars for a long time?"

"I think yes – he should be able to do that – but he being one of the prime opposition leaders and the 'Tool Kit' already rolled out by him – there would be mass protests and government as well the courts would grant him a bail releasing him and he would then tamper with evidence..." Priya raised her eyebrows in concern when he said this... "So what do you think – should we let them kill him or show these proofs to Mr Mahal?"

"Chaits – since when did you start with these thoughts? Though they are doing the right things – they are doing it the wrong way – I would like to go legally first..." Priya wondered what had come over Chaitanya.

"You are right – we will make copies as usual and hand these over to Mr Mahal in the morning and see what he can do about it and what Rajkumar plans to do and if *Akhand Hind Fauj* is able to do what they said ... they have given a challenge to IB and other agencies... yes – we will give this file to Mr Mahal. That sorts the matter – let's sleep over it and be at Mr Mahal's office tomorrow morning – I don't know where their command centre is..."

"Ok – good night – and if you feel pain or are uncomfortable let me know – we will go back to the hospital..."

And they slept off – to be ready for a big day...

CHAPTER TWENTY-FOUR

TWENTY FOUR

The morning awakened them with thoughts of what was going to happen during the day. They reached Mr Mahal's office as planned and he was waiting for them to arrive.

"I spoke to Rajkumar – that idiot thinks this is a ploy by the government to stop his rally... so he will be present at the rally – we estimate a crowd of around 100 Thousand and we are putting around 1000 operatives – both male and female at the venue – approximately every operative will look after 100 people there. We have already started to install CCTV cameras at various locations and to add to that we will have 6 drones with camera who would beam the footage LIVE to the command centre where you would be placed to identify. Priya – take some other cameraman with you to the venue and be amongst the crowd of women that are attending this rally – apart from the one that you or channel gives you – you will have another high performance microphone on you. You will try and speak to anyone who Chaitanya thinks could be the 'Capt Laxmi Sehgal' and if he identifies her – our team will take over and arrest her... You both got what you have to do?"

They nodded in unision and parted ways – she to her studio and Chaitanya to the command centre...

At command centre – the guy explained them how the cameras will be placed with each camera having a number and similarly where the LIVE footage of drones could be seen. They had their lunch by the time many of the CCTV cameras had been put up and they were going LIVE one by one – the drone cameras were activated and had a trial run – Chaitanya was getting used to the surveillance that was being put up for Rajkumar though he hated him for his anti-India stance and his greed for power.

The crowd had started trickling in by 4PM and even as he sipped on the tea – his vision was fixed on all cameras' LIVE footage to identify a patriot who wanted to save India...

Around 4.30PM almost all the crowd who was supposed to be present were at the venue – almost about 1.5 lakh. It was like an ocean of people who had gathered there for the rally. Few carried pipes and horns which they were blowing shrill – mostly they belonged to Rajkumar's party who wanted to stimulate the crowd that had gathered there...

"Ask your person to speak to the 3rd woman in the 4th row – she is approximately the same shape ..." Chaitanya said trying to recognize Capt Laxmi Sehgal. The person in charge of the mission asked someone to speak to the woman on his radio system ... the woman was stout and healthy – she seemed strong and stood straight.

"Sir – are you wanting me to speak with me? – I am that woman who you are pointing to..."

"Shit – wrong number – but one thing is now clear – Capt Laxmi Sehgal is like a soldier and she has a build somewhat like this woman cadre of yours..." Chaitanya focused on other cameras to identify her... He looked at a drone camera, "Stop – that's Capt Abid Hasan..."

The person in charge asked to revert to the location of the drone – Capt Abid Hasan had vanished into the crowd

– changed his position in the ocean of crowd. They started to rewind the footage and Chaitanya saw him again in the recorded footage – "That's him" he said pointing, "That's Capt Abid Hasan..."

"Are you sure of that?"

"100% - that's him..."

"Send the snap to every operative there – I want him alive." Mr Mahal said and the orders followed as well the photo sent to every operative at the venue. They only had to wait till he was apprehended.

"Where is Priya – I don't see her ... she might be in danger because they know her and could pose a problem ... Ah! There she is with her microphone... I will request you to keep an eye on her lest these people abduct her and try to negotiate their escape..." Chaitanya kept on scanning from one screen to another... "Hey – stop – ask Priya to speak to the woman in 8th row standing 7th from right..."

Priya was in the same row to get a better view of the rally – she quickly moved toward the woman spotted by Chaitanya, "Hi – what do you think of this rally?" she posed a question as if she is on reporting LIVE and interviewing the crowd...

"This is not a good rally – Rajkumar doesn't have enough points to convince the crowd..." the woman who seemed to be his party worker replied.

"No – that's not her voice..." Chaitanya was multitasking – looking at the screen trying to identify her and listening to the voices of women who he was pointing at... 'That's another one who could be her..." he pointed. A female operative approached her and collided with her – the woman started to swear at the operative – "Not her too ... that's not her voice..." and he kept scanning various screens. "Ask Priya to talk to the woman at the edge where the crowd seems to be scattered around in the 9th row..." even as Rajkumar made an entry to the venue and the crowd cheered – many horns and pipes were blown for his reception.

Priya had some trouble crossing the crowd and going to the edge where the woman stood, "What do you make of this rally?" she asked her.

"Who is interested in the rally – I came here because I was offered money to attend this rally – 500 rupees to come here and 500 rupees to cheer him as our leader – that's big money for person like me..."

"That's not her too – I wonder where she could be hiding in this vast bought out crowd – I don't know how many people he has paid to come here..." Chaitanya remarked.

"Carry on with your search – I want to nab at least one of them to know how their organization works and who all operate the organization..." Mr Mahal prodded him to go on with the search.

Rajkumar in the din of noise climbed up the ramp and greeted the crowd in a sign of V... and the noise drained down – the crowd waiting for him to speak... Priya had now reached further away from the stage, from where Rajkumar was addressing the crowd – she had covered initial rows where Chaitanya thought Capt Laxmi Sehgal was located – she was now on 52nd row...

"I am not afraid of the government – the government is afraid of me. I will carry on with my work. Let me tell you what happened today morning..." Rajkumar was now addressing the rally, "I was trying to gather information on what is happening in India – when the Chief of IB walks into my home. He suggests me that I should avoid coming to today's rally because some fictional group who call themselves as patriots want to kill me – such is the fear of me in the government that they are using any and every means to stop my progress."

He looked around to see the reaction of the crowd – meanwhile at the command centre – Chaitanya was furiously looking at the live footage by CCTV cameras and the drones to identify Capt Laxmi Sehgal and to locate Capt Abid Hasan – both seemed to evade his eyes... He saw a probable female in the 54th row and asked Priya to interview her – Priya reached the location – it was the edge of the crowd and the barricades ended – from there the ground was open and people were huge in numbers, scattered on that ground behind those barricades. Chaitanya suddenly recalled how Rafique Shaikh was killed and told his concern to Mr Mahal who was assured that terraces of all buildings nearby with a sight on Rajkumar were occupied by IB's Special Forces and there was not a single chance that anyone could snipe him out... Priya approached that woman and started to interview her – Chaitanya immediately rejected that she could not be the one ... he kept searching the crowd...

Rajkumar turned to his 'Tool Kit' – "The government is the enemy of minorities – it wants to take away all the rights that protect the minorities... the government wants to persecute the minorities..." before he could go on – he fell to the ground and had a fit of spasms ... the IB team near to the stage rushed on to the stage and informed the command centre that he had been hit by dart – maybe a poisonous dart in his neck...

"Stop the crowd that is inside the barricades – let the people who are behind go securely – ensure that there's no stampede – take Rajkumar to the nearest hospital." Mr Mahal briefed the team that was present at the venue, "He should have heeded the word of IB." he said turning to Chaitanya.

Chaitanya could see that there was a stampede behind the barricades – Priya was standing near the end of barricade at the back when he had last talked to her. He called her but her phone was switched off – he told the command centre coordinator to call her – all they could hear was the din of the on-going stampede. He informed that Priya was either missing or hurt in the stampede and Mr Mahal ordered his team to be on lookout for her... Now there were 2 actions before IB – one was to identify who killed Rajkumar and second – where was Priya...

Chaitanya kept scanning the cameras again and again to see her safe. The drones had now been recalled as there was no need for their surveillance. Chaitanya was getting more and more worried as he could not see Priya and her phone was switched off from the time he had called her last – was she safe? – was the only question he had in his mind...

IB stopped all those who were carrying pipes and trumpets – only they could have hit Rajkumar with a dart. The others were scanned and let out and this was taking time. There were people who were hurt in the stampede – it was a tough task to isolate them and move them to the hospital – Priya was not amongst them. About 4 hours from the time, Rajkumar was killed, suddenly his phone rang – it was Priya...

"Priya – where are you? – are you safe?" Chaitanya asked in anxiety.

"Yes – I am safe – is Rajkumar alive?" she asked and he was confused. If Priya didn't know of Rajkumar's death – where the hell was she?

"Where are you – I am coming to get you – tell me the location."

"I am at the Palam Airport – I got to tell you something..."

"Later – I am coming there to see that you are safe and bring you back safely of the command centre..." he said and told Mr Mahal of her location. Mr Mahal arranged for a vehicle with IB Special Force squad following them and he rushed through the Delhi traffic to Palam Airport. He saw Priya waiting for him at Ambience Mall entrance near the airport. He rushed out of the vehicle and hugged her for he could see that she was safe.

"How come you reached the airport – you were supposed to be at the rally of Rajkumar..."

"I met one of the friends of my informer when I was interviewing the lady at the back of the barricades. He said that whatever happens will happen at the Rally – but my informer wanted to give me some important information and he had come to take her to the location where the information would be given... after all, I can watch what happened on TV – I had already reached the edge of the barricaded crowd – so I followed him outside the place of the rally – the police on guard recognized me and let us pass through. Once outside, we went to a waiting cab which brought us to the airport..."

"Why was your phone switched off and where did you throw the microphones?"

"The microphones could have been lost somewhere in the crowd. The guy said that my phone could have been tapped and our location could be compromised – he put his phone off and took mine and put it off too and kept both the phones with him. He didn't speak much – just kept asking me like a normal person would as to how I work – how much glamour is in my work – is my work difficult... He said that he had to take a flight and got off at the airport and asked me to travel to Ambience Mall – I will get the information and phone there. He asked me to while my time away in the mall since the information was on its way and may take an hour or so for the person to get that to me."

"Did anyone give you the information – because I doubt that the person wanted to take you away from that venue – so that we, together won't be able to identify anyone..."

"I had a wait of about 4-5 hours in the Mall and had nothing much to do – so I started shopping the items that were on my list. Around 4-5 hours later, a teenage boy approached me and gave me a packet saying that it contained the information. I opened the packet and found my phone and another USB in there... The boy was gone – vanished in the crowd. That's when I turned my phone on and called you..."

"Oh! You had me scared – come let's go to the Command Centre where Mr Mahal is waiting for us..." he grabbed her hand and led her to the vehicle and signalled to the men from IB that all is well. Once at the Command Centre, they met Mr Mahal and relayed all that had happened. They informed her that Rajkumar had been killed by a poisonous dart. Mr Mahal informed them that all people with pipes and trumpets had been arrested and being questioned by IB.

"Let's get back to the recordings of the rally and you try and identify that man called Capt Abid Hasan..." Mr Mahal suggested. And Chaitanya went back along with Mr Mahal and Priya to where the recording was being played back to them... Chaitanya started to scan the recordings...

"There he is – Capt Abid Hasan..." he pointed out again.

"He is the guy who led me to the informer teen and the USB." Priya pointed out the same person.

"Oh – that means – it was Capt Abid Hasan to lead you to the airport side Mall. The teen boy must be a part of their group – *Akhand Hind Fauj* – who gave you the USB and your phone..."

"Now that we have a face from that group – the group will soon be identified..." Mr Mahal said with satisfaction on his face.

"Don't count chickens before they are hatched, Mr Mahal – we need to find out where he has disappeared after leaving Priya at the Mall..."

"You are right – I will post operatives who will search the area as well the CCTV footage at the airport and tell us his whereabouts..." Mr Mahal said with conviction that he has found one solid clue and that clue will lead to the arrest of the entire group. Chaitanya's phone buzzed – it was a land line...

"Hi – release the people IB is holding – they have nothing to do with Rajkumar's killing – it was us who plotted and executed his killing." Chaitanya recognized Capt Laxmi Sehgal's voice which carried on, "Don't look for Capt Abid Hasan as well – he has taken a flight to a destination outside India on a mission – his flight has landed 2 hours ago and he is safe from you – but our next target is in danger – he is already on his way to the target..."

"Who is the next target?"

"You belong to NEWS, don't you? – Wait for the sensational NEWS item – from Pakistan – in due course you will get the information. Be sure you all don't blow his cover – he is going to do something that will make India more secure and proud."

"How do I know that one of the people apprehended by IB wasn't your person?"

"Capt Abid Hasan was deliberately sent to the venue as a decoy. You kept looking for him on the ground and forgot to look at the sky. You had 6 drones monitoring the venue – but you failed to notice that there was a 7th drone which also was hovering over the venue – we shot the poisonous dart from that drone – our person who was operating that drone had a unerring aim and we finished Rajkumar without being at the location..."

"Must acknowledge the planning..." Chaitanya said wondering at the deceptive attack by them.

"Now that Rajkumar's chapter is closed – check the USB and tell Mr Mahal – if action is not taken – there will be more killings – at least a million of them... Bye – we will keep in touch..." and she hung up her call. Chaitanya had kept his phone on loud speaker of the phone and Mr Mahal was listening. He shook his head and asked the people caught on suspicion to be released.

"I am hungry – let's go to the mess we normally meet and have our dinner. Then we will discuss on how to deal with their new threat of killing a million people..." Mr Mahal suggested.

After they finished their dinner, Mr Mahal looking at Chaitanya's laptop suggested to have a look at the USB. Chaitanya attached the USB and made a copy of the USB before opening the contents... It contained 3 files – one in word and 2 XL sheets. Chaitanya opened the word file...

'There are 2 XL sheets containing – one – Names of leaders and people involved in legalising the presence of Bangladeshi, Rohingya and Pakistani fugitives by allotting them legal documents like Ration cards and Aadhar cards – thus legally converting them into Indian citizens.

The other XL sheet contains Original Names and addresses of these refugees and their recent names and recent addresses in which they are registered as Indian citizens. Some of them are sleeper cells of ISI.

IB gets 15 days within which they have to arrest the leaders and people who are legalising these migrants and round up as many refugees they can lay their hands on and deport them back to their countries – if IB fails – we will start killing whoever is left and it's up to the Government to explain the killings on this mass scale. If we get more data – we will let you know. This is keeping the promise made to Chaitanya that Government agencies should have chance before we start our killing spree.' This was the message of the group with its Tiger logo on the top right...

They looked at the XL sheets – the people legalising these refugees were close to 75000 and the refugee list had at least a million names – it was a daunting task for IB.

CHAPTER TWENTY-FIVE

TWENTY FIVE

Chaitanya left the USB with Mr Mahal and then left with Priya to their home. He was okay but the torture by Mr Das still had some pains left. He said that he will take a leave till he feels better to join the channel back...

He was tired of all the running around and really wanted to rest. Priya suggested that he visit the orphanage where he had been brought up – change of the location will help him in his recovery. She said she will be okay and wait for his return while she will continue working with the channel as a NEWS presenter which will not expose her to danger... So Chaitanya left for the orphanage and she requested her editor and told him her plans to present NEWS till Chaitanya returned and the editor knowing the danger she was in, agreed...

In about 2 weeks, Chaitanya returned from the orphanage, relaxed and refreshed. He had another day to go and wondered if IB had been successful in arresting those leaders and the people who were doing the dirty job of legalising the refugees. He was not concerned about the refugees – they had no place in India in the first place as well he had seen those refugees run from behind the mosque at Jalori gate and thought they deserved what was in store for them...

He had a day or two of leave left and was still relaxing and thinking about wedding bells with Priya who was in the NEWS room when his phone buzzed. It was Mr Mahal who called him to his office. He lazily got up freshened up and left for Mr Mahal's office... He had a small wait as Mr Mahal was busy with some important official work. He entered his cabin...

"Welcome – young man, are you now feeling better and raring to go?" was his first question.

"Yes Sir – had a good time at the orphanage I grew up."

"Good – do you still dream of appearing for the army test next year?"

"Yes Sir – I do..."

"Well – your wait is over. You will not be joining the army but Special Security Forces of IB – the same training will be given as that of army but you will serve in my department and protect the nation. Is it okay with you?"

Chaitanya couldn't believe his ears and he was overwhelmed by this offer by Mr Mahal, "Yes Sir – I am ready and raring to go whenever you say..."

"Good – We saw your capabilities and your thought process and it matches or sometimes exceeds that of a normal IB personnel and that's why we chose you to join us – welcome aboard..."

"Thank you Sir." Chaitanya couldn't contain his excitement at this offer, "Would you mind if I tell Priya of this appointment?"

"Yes – of course – you are going to get married, aren't you? – she has every right to know about this appointment – but you will say to her and everyone else that you are joining Indian Army not IB – Lt. Chaitanya – here this is your appointment letter – sign it – hey! Read what's written in that letter first..."

"No need – I trust you and I know you will always think for my better future – I am signing it..."

"Good – you have 3 months to join IMA for training. Get married before that – you will be at IMA and as a soldier who will receive tough army training for 1 year and then after that you will join IB with all required Army skills – you will have additional 1 year of IB training. And – now if you say that **Akhand Hind Fauj** is correct in their deeds – I can now Court Martial you... do you understand?"

"Yes – Sir." Chaitanya said beaming with joy.

"Okay – Now go and prepare your joining in 3 months and get married – else you will be stuck for 2-3 years before you get time to get married and maybe with no leaves for your honeymoon..." Mr Mahal smiled, "All the best."

He couldn't contain his excitement and called Priya to the same expensive restaurant where they had met Mr Das. The treat was on him for this news. Priya had one more bulletin before she could be free to meet him – he had already proceeded to the restaurant. He booked a table and was sitting there when an old couple approached him and asked him if they can sit while a table gets free for them. He knew Priya would be taking some time so he nodded to them to occupy the seats on his table.

"Thank you young man..." said the old woman accepting his generous seat – a voice he recognized as that belonging to Capt Laxmi Sehgal, "Don't look too astonished – this is a makeup done by a professional. We want to speak to you."

Chaitanya was aware that the old man seated next to him had a gun in his hand hidden away in his muffler and pointing at him.

"Don't you think 15 days is a low time frame to act upon a million people and arrest them – you gave just about 15 days to IB to apprehend those refugees?"

"No – they have various means and the entire police force is at their disposal for this work – while we have to depend upon our own resources – IB has massive manpower for doing this job."

"One more question – what if the people of India choose to elect such corrupt leaders and traitors to power and send them to assembly or the parliament?"

"I will say – People of India deserve who they have chosen to elect and suffer – but we will keep doing our job – cleaning India of these corrupt leaders and traitors – nothing will deter us and we are unbiased – whether the person is with the ruling party or in the opposition – he is a minister in a state or even if he is the Prime Minister – they all will be dealt the same way – they will be killed – unless IB arrests them and sends them to jail..."

"Why kill them?"

"Listen – as per our promise to you – we have started giving information to the IB. We are giving sufficient time for IB and other agencies to act – but if they fail to act – we will act. After all, we are working for the same goal – cleaning India of culprits and traitors... I would have loved if you would have joined us – but it is okay if you are with IB – it will make our communication easier."

"How do you know that I am joining IB?"

"Well young man, we have our informers everywhere – be it government or underworld – we know everything that goes on ... anyways, we will take your leave – it's almost time for your girlfriend to arrive... be in touch. And what I will suggest – we give the information to you – as IB, you take action and if you feel the person would escape the judiciary – you let us know – we will fix him – now that's a good deal, isn't it? – Think about it – you have 2 years of your training to think about this... Bye..." Saying thus the old couple got out of their seats and saying that the place was too crowded for their 50 anniversary they left the place leaving behind a bewildered Chaitanya.

Priya entered the restaurant and was eager to know why he had called her there and why he was footing the bill. He said he will let her know later and to have a fantastic dinner. They had a fantastic dinner and rode to their home. He then told her of the offer Mr Mahal had made and that he had decided to join the Army. She was very happy for him and kissed him in appreciation of his achievement. Then they discussed about their wedding and how they would have to talk to her parents for this wedding and get their approval. Also how they had to take time out for their honeymoon before he joins IMA for his training and started making plans for the honeymoon...

She suddenly looked coy at him and said, "I still have few of those special pills left – how about letting your to be wife know, how you will love her?"

He lifted her off her feet and carried her into the bedroom.

Acknowledgements

Thank You for Reading this story and we do hope that this did entertain you and made you think...

We at 'BakBak' (YouTube Channel) are glad to be associated with Prasad Deshpande and we take pride in promoting his amazingly different concept stories... This channel is for the dialogs and scenes that were edited and couldn't make it to the print because his stories are in English and these are either in other languages or not in line with stories.

Channel link: **@ BakBak-ui4fw**

His other published books are as given below...

The Conducer

My Fiancée's Boyfriend

Red Clipper

Disposables

The Tempest – a short story

To get to his stories just type "**prasad deshpande**" on Amazon...

We are planning to launch his best of the stories in coming months...

Wait for it...

We request you to send your feedback to the email ...

pdsspartners @ gmail.com

Or, Follow the Author Pages managed by us and his close friends...

Instagram - @ pen2me

Facebook/thiscanhappentoyou

(Seen as "Flights of Fantasy")

For his other very short and other free works you can follow his account on Facebook ...

Facebook/pen2me

.... a "BakBak" promotion

www.ingramcontent.com/pod-product-compliance
Lightning Source LLC
LaVergne TN
LVHW090406210926
848480LV00002B/465
9798890664822